お野菜

乳製品

FISH

カット野菜

MY HERO ACADEMIA

SCHOOL BRIEFS

1

1-A: Parents' Day

ORIGINAL CONCEPT BY
KOHEI HORIKOSHI

WRITTEN BY
ANRI YOSHI

U.A. HIGH SCHOOL

Hero Course: Class 1-A

Izuku Midoriya

Birthday: July 15
Quirk: One For All

Katsuki Bakugo

Birthday: April 20
Quirk: Explosion

Shoto Todoroki

Birthday: January 11
Quirk:
Half-Cold Half-Hot

Tenya Ida

Birthday: August 22
Quirk: Engine

Fumikage Tokoyami

Birthday: October 30
Quirk: Dark Shadow

Minoru Mineta

Birthday: October 8
Quirk: Pop Off

Ochaco Uraraka

Birthday:
December 27
Quirk: Zero Gravity

Momo Yaoyorozu

Birthday:
September 23
Quirk: Creation

Tsuyu Asui

Birthday: February 12
Quirk: Frog

Yuga Aoyama

Birthday: May 30
Quirk: Navel Laser

Mina Ashido

Birthday: July 30
Quirk: Acid

Mashirao Ojiro

Birthday: May 28
Quirk: Tail

Denki Kaminari

Birthday: June 29
Quirk: Electrification

Eijiro Kirishima

Birthday: October 16
Quirk: Hardening

Koji Koda

Birthday: February 1
Quirk: Anivoice

Rikido Sato

Birthday: June 19
Quirk: Sugar Rush

STUDENTS & FACULTY ROLL CALL

Mezo Shoji

Birthday: February 15
Quirk: Dupli-Arms

Kyoka Jiro

Birthday: August 1
Quirk: Earphone Jack

Hanta Sero

Birthday: July 28
Quirk: Tape

Toru Hagakure

Birthday: June 16
Quirk: Invisibility

Hero Course: Faculty

All Might

Birthday: June 10
Quirk: One For All

Shota Aizawa

Birthday: November 8
Quirk: Erasure

Thirteen

Birthday: February 3
Quirk: Black Hole

Cementoss

Birthday: March 22
Quirk: Cement

Midnight

Birthday: March 9
Quirk: Somnambulist

Ectoplasm

Birthday: March 23
Quirk: Clones

Present Mic

Birthday: July 7
Quirk: Voice

Nezu

Birthday: January 1
Quirk: High Specs

STORY

People in this world possess exceptional abilities called "Quirks." Some use their Quirks in pursuit of peace, while others choose to commit crimes with their powers, but they're all part of the same superpowered society. Izuku Midoriya may have been born Quirkless, but he nonetheless gets into U.A. High School, an academy for heroes in training. There, he walks the path toward becoming a true hero! The stories in this book offer a heretofore unrevealed glimpse at the everyday lives of the students attending U.A. High.

MY HERO ACADEMIA
SCHOOL BRIEFS
1

1-A: Parents' Day

CONTENTS

It happened in an instant. No sooner had the villain in the black cape and mask released the lighter into the pit than a roaring blaze exploded forth, as if from the very gates of hell. Buffeted by the blast of hot air, the students of class 1-A flinched in spite of themselves. They stood frozen in place, eyes locked desperately on the flames, forced to bear the screams coming from the cage.

The cage that held their parents.

Izuku Midoriya's eyes always held a certain strength—he was hoping to become a hero, after all— and now that strength burned even brighter, fanned by the flames.

"Izuku!"

"Mom!"

The boy's mother shouted for help, extending her hand from within the cage, and Midoriya reached out instinctively. But between them was a field of fire, sturdy iron bars, and a villain.

It had all begun two weeks earlier...

Part 2
Notice from School

Internships were over, and the students were spending the placid days between spring and summer preparing for their term exams.

"Next. Midoriya."

Aizawa's unconcerned voice echoed across the ruined cityscape. Seemingly without a care in the world, class 1-A's homeroom teacher peered up through his long, unkempt hair at a group of his students. The kids perched on the third floor of a building that was on the verge of collapse.

"Okay," came the nervous reply from Izuku Midoriya, a freckled boy with an unruly mop of hair and distinctly plain features. "Good luck, Deku!" Ochaco Uraraka's face poked out from within the line of girls behind Midoriya. At Uraraka's smile and cheery encouragement, he turned bright red, murmured "Mhm!" and stepped into a tube leading to the ground below. The emergency chute warped under Midoriya's weight as he slid down; the perfect tool for evacuating tall buildings, it was as simple to use as any playground slide.

This was U.A. High School, and class 1-A of the school's Hero Course was in the midst of Basic Hero Training. Their sprawling campus was home to a number of facilities, including a stadium that could seat tens of thousands and even the Unforeseen Simulation Joint—U.S.J. for short—which provided heroes in training with simulations of myriad natural disasters. The League of Villains had attacked U.S.J. recently, and memories of the incident were fresh in the students' minds as they drilled in a derelict urban zone, also on school grounds.

|A|

The advent of Quirks seemed like some ancient happening, but it was still relatively recent history. At the start, people viewed the rare special abilities as supernatural phenomena. Miracles on earth, even. However, the extraordinary became increasingly ordinary over the generations, until about 80 percent of the population possessed what had come to be called Quirks. Sadly, there was never a shortage of those who opted to use those powers for evil. Crime surged. Chaos reigned. Law and order crumbled. But it didn't take long for a different breed of empowered individuals to fight back and protect society from those who would menace it.

Heroes.

Guardians of the meek, foils to the mighty, agents of justice. A profession that humanity could only dream of in ages past left the realm of fantasy and became reality. With public support, those early heroes gained legal rights of their own along with official systems to govern them. Nations compensated heroes for their contributions to society, and society elevated them as a new class of celebrity.

Still, it was never the case that just anyone could

become a hero, and even in the present, those hoping to take up the cape or cowl would first have to prove themselves qualified. To preserve order in the brave new world, use of Quirks by nonheroes in public spaces was quickly outlawed on principle, meaning that hero hopefuls needed government approval in the form of a special license before they could freely wield their powers. To that end, specialized courses of study and hero schools emerged to teach students the fundamentals needed to earn those licenses. Naturally, few challengers were up to the task, and even fewer made it through the trials of that apex of hero education, U.A. High.

Izuku Midoriya was Quirkless, a rare sort in the modern era. Every hero needs a Quirk, and latent Quirks are sure to present by age four if at all; Midoriya had had to confront this cruel pair of truths on his own fourth birthday. His dream of becoming a hero like All Might—the current top hero—always seemed painfully out of reach, and though Midoriya had never quite lost all hope, his dream had earned him plenty of sneers and scorn along the way.

As it happened, a chance encounter with All Might

saw Midoriya's wish fulfilled. His idol had glimpsed a certain something in the boy and put him through hellish training before transferring to him All Might's own Quirk, "One For All," a power passed down from hero to hero in secret over multiple generations. At first, every use of his new, unwieldy power left Midoriya maimed by the recoil, but thanks to his classes at U.A. and lessons from All Might's own teacher, Gran Torino, he was finally on the road to controlling his Quirk.

U

"Hup."

After a moment of near free fall, Midoriya popped out of the evacuation chute.

"Great, boys are done. Girls next. Come on down, Yaoyorozu."

"Yes, Sensei," replied Momo Yaoyorozu, diving feet-first into the tube.

On the ground, the short, lumpy-headed Minoru Mineta seemed poised and ready for the class's vice president to touch down, but he let out a forceful sigh when she did.

"What's wrong, Mineta?" asked Midoriya, prompting another sigh from his classmate.

"C'mon, man. Girls coming down slides? That should mean upskirt views! But everyone's in these dumb gym uniforms... I mean, I knew we would be, but still! No justice in this world when a guy can't even peep up a skirt or two!"

"Let us know when you grow up, Mineta," came the retort from Tsuyu Asui, the frog-faced girl who descended next.

"She's quite right, Mineta. I fail to see how flipped skirts would improve our training. This athletic wear is geared towards mobility, making it the logical choice for an evacuation exercise. No, wait now! In any genuine evacuation, I suspect we would, in fact, witness a number of women in skirts. I see... Skirts would add a dash of realism!"

The ever-serious Tenya Ida seemed taken aback at having convinced himself of Mineta's position, until, with a concerned smile, Midoriya said, "Nah, I don't think it works that way." Midoriya had been intimi-

dated by the overly earnest Ida when they'd first met at U.A.'s entrance exam, but the two had become good friends in the time since.

"Wipe that dumb grin off your sorry excuse for a face, Deku."

"Really, Kacchan…?" replied Midoriya to the barbed comment. It had come from Katsuki Bakugo, who now glared at him from a few paces away. Midoriya was plenty used to verbal abuse and more from his childhood "friend," but things had gotten better since high school had started, as Bakugo now found himself surrounded by classmates less willing to put up with his eternal bad attitude. Well, "better" was relative when it came to Bakugo.

"Evac training is just the pits, is all."

"How can you say that? Any hero worth his salt must be ready to prioritize the rescue at any time! Learning how to utilize lifesaving tools such as this one is key, making this a wholly worthwhile lesson!"

"Like I care. We all got our strengths, y'know? Let someone else handle the rescues while I kick some villain ass."

"Do you truly hope to become a hero someday?"

Ida's strong sense of justice was at constant odds with Bakugo's particular brand of arrogance, and Midoriya forced himself to step in as the spat escalated.

"Take it easy, Ida!"

"He's not wrong about people having different strengths," muttered Shoto Todoroki, a boy with an old burn covering a swath of his stony face.

"You think so, Todoroki?"

"I just mean it's hard to picture Bakugo saving anyone."

"Try saying that again!"

"No doubt! He'd probably hurt 'em even worse!" agreed an enthusiastic Denki Kaminari.

"How about I make you my first 'rescue' then!" shot back Bakugo as a small explosion burst from the palm of his hand—a product of the nitroglycerin-like sweat afforded him by his Quirk.

The last of the girls had popped out of the chute. Some stared at the squabbling boys, shocked and dismissive, while others moved in to stop the fighting. In the end, it was their teacher's composed voice that did it.

"Have you all forgotten why you're here?"

The students of class 1-A snapped to attention at the sound of Aizawa's gravelly reprimand. Their teacher believed in rationality above all else, and the past few months had made them wary of this side of him.

Aizawa's typically listless eyes opened wide in a flash of red. The man also went by "Erasure Hero: Eraser Head," as his Quirk allowed him to "erase" other Quirks; whomever he stared at would have their Quirk nullified until the next time Aizawa blinked. Not very famous as far as professional heroes went, he made a point of avoiding media exposure, lest it interfere with his work.

The kids piped down, and the energy left Aizawa's eyes.

"Different strengths or not, excuses like that won't cut it once you're on the scene. Pro heroes willingly do whatever they can to help."

He scanned his students and continued.

"When the police and rescue teams can't make it in time, it's up to you to point evacuees towards safety."

"Isn't is faster to save them for real, instead of just guiding them or whatever?"

One sleeve of Toru Hagakure's gym uniform curved

upward, indicating a raised hand. Her Quirk made her invisible, so her clothing always appeared to be floating in midair.

"I believe Sensei is referring to mass evacuations?"

Aizawa confirmed Yaoyorozu's suspicion with a curt nod and went on.

"Exactly. Saving one or two people is one thing, but these rescue tools are invaluable when dealing with a larger group. You don't want to find yourselves lacking the knowledge to use them when the time comes, which is why their basic application is part of our curriculum. Understood, Bakugo?"

Singled out by name, Bakugo uttered "Sure"—a huge concession for him.

Nearby, Midoriya gave a small gasp and began muttering furiously to himself.

"Of course! And I bet we could even combine these rescue tools with our Quirks in order to deal with mass evacuations! Like Uraraka's ability to make things float, or Sero's tape... Even Mineta's sticky balls could be useful. A professional hero should be ready to come up with all sorts of clever combinations on the fly!"

Aiming to be a pro, Midoriya was a die-hard hero

fanboy who never stopped taking notes, mental or otherwise. At first, his classmates had been horrified when he would fall into a trance and start thinking out loud, but by now everyone had come to accept his odd habit, Bakugo aside.

"Anyhow, next up is…"

But Aizawa was cut off by a roar from above as his dumfounded students watched a helicopter descend on their position. A massive figure leaped from the door, nearly blotting out the sun as he fell.

"I am here…from the sky!"

"All Might, is that you?!"

The number one hero's rippling muscles hit the ground and shook the earth. The pair of forelocks shooting straight up from his brow swayed gently in the helicopter's wake. A broad grin exposed his gleaming white teeth.

"So sorry I'm late, everyone! I was on my way when—wouldn't you know it?—a pesky villain turned up, just begging to be dealt with!"

"Unbelievable. This was supposed to be your class to teach."

Unlike the exasperated Aizawa, Midoriya practically had stars in his eyes.

"I saw the news online during lunch! You really caught a bank robber?"

"Indeed, but what hasn't made the news yet is that another ne'er-do-well was holed up inside the bank."

"T-too awesome, All Might!"

When it came to idolizing heroes and their deeds, Midoriya wore his excitement on his sleeve, and All Might, in particular, was a cut above the rest in his mind. Like a force of nature, the hero's mere existence had brought crime rates down. His nickname, "Symbol of Peace," was no overstatement.

Ever since All Might had granted his power to Midoriya, the two had become master and pupil, but only a small handful of people were privy to this secret. The public was also unaware that the hero's true form was a shrunken shell of skin and bones, and that he could only bulk up and play the part of hero for an increasingly limited amount of time each day.

"Midoriya, praise is always appreciated, but let's shelve it for now. We wouldn't want to keep the chopper waiting, would we?"

"The helicopter? You mean it wasn't just bringing you here…?"

"There's no emergency, kid. And I'd never use it just to make a grand entrance. No, the helicopter is part of your rescue training! Prepare yourselves!"

"The H-Hero Course sure is s-something else…" stammered an impressed Midoriya.

UA

After a bit of rescue training on a snowcapped mountain and then by the waterfront, the students returned to the classroom.

"If I ever drown, I wanna get CPR from a chick… Hot, heavy, and deep. Enough to take my breath away!"

"Wouldn't that defeat the point?"

As Mineta and Kaminari chatted, Fumikage Tokoyami mumbled, "Truly, an embodiment of lustful desires…" from a few seats away. The bird-headed boy's Quirk was "Dark Shadow," and it granted him a retractable, shadowy familiar eternally bound to his body.

Aizawa entered the classroom, and everyone

straightened in their seats.

"Good work today. Moving right along, we'll be having Parents' Day next week."

The students clamored at Aizawa's announcement.

"Even the Hero Course has gotta do stuff like that?" yelped Eijiro Kirishima, a stouthearted boy whose Quirk enabled him to harden any part of his body. Aizawa ignored the groans and grumbles and distributed a stack of handouts.

"Make sure your parents or guardians see this. And for homework, you'll be writing them letters of appreciation."

At this, the class grew silent for a moment before exploding with laughter.

"Hang on, hang on. What're we, little kids?"

Everyone began to agree with the outspoken Kaminari, but their teacher cut them off.

"Have I ever been one to joke?"

Aizawa's rhetorical question returned the room to silence.

"During the class, you will each read your letters aloud to your parents."

It dawned on the students just how serious their

teacher was, and they couldn't conceal their discomfort.

"For real? That's ridiculous!"

"Talk about embarrassing…"

Ida shot up above the commotion, began swinging his arms about—as he was wont to do—and shouted.

"Everyone, quiet down! Quiet! Quiet!"

"You're louder than anyone else, Ida," said Asui, sitting in front of Ida.

"Oh. Apologies. However, surely you understand why we're all so vexed, Sensei? Parents' Day implies an ordinary class that our parents or guardians come to observe, so I can't understand why we would instead be reading letters of appreciation! Shouldn't they bear witness to an activity more befitting the Hero Course?"

Aizawa responded to Ida's self-assured thoughts on the matter. "Nothing would be a better fit for the Hero Course."

"What do you mean, Sensei…?"

The teacher surveyed his class and went on.

"As aspiring heroes, you're all bound to receive thanks and appreciation from those you save. Which is why it's essential to consider just what that entails. Well, not that you all becoming pros is necessarily set in stone."

"How true! This exercise will confirm whether or not we have the correct frame of mind to be heroes, who must remain modest, humble, and always grateful! That makes perfect sense!"

"You didn't take much convincing," laughed Uraraka from the seat behind Ida. The earnest boy's quick change of attitude drew strained chuckles from the whole class, which was now in a much more accepting mood. Anything was possible in the Hero Course, so they couldn't very well let this one assignment fluster them.

"Before the recitations, though, we'll give them a brief tour of the campus and a practical demo."

"Shouldn't that be the main event?" blurted out Kaminari, asking the question on everyone's mind.

"Parents' Day, huh? And what do we do about these letters?"

"No choice but to write them," said Todoroki to a troubled Midoriya.

Ida, also walking with the two boys, voiced his own thoughts. "I had my doubts at first, but now it seems like a fantastic idea. Naturally we feel grateful to our families for all they do, but rarely do we get a chance to express that in words. I wonder if there's a page limit? Too short, and I'm afraid I won't be able to fit all my feelings into the letter."

The three boys were walking home, still in uniform, and at a glance, they might've looked like your average teenagers—but nothing was further from the truth. Though the public was none the wiser, these three had in fact battled the Hero Killer, Stain, a villain who had terrorized society.

However, only pro heroes were permitted to use Quirks with the intent of causing bodily harm, so by fighting the fiend in public, the boys had broken the rules. In the eyes of the law, it normally wouldn't matter that their opponent was a murderer who slaughtered in the name of "purifying" society, but the powers that be had decided to let it slide, lest the blot on their records ruin the futures of the three potential heroes.

As it happened, Ida had been out for revenge on Stain, who'd maimed the boy's respected brother, while Midoriya and Todoroki had shown up to keep Ida from meeting the same fate. Ever since the battle, these three had shared an unspoken bond.

"Wow, Ida. You think you'll be writing that much…? I can't even imagine how to start. I mean, I'm always leaving comments on heroes' websites, but an actual letter is a different story."

"Is that so? I find myself writing thank-you cards now and again."

"For what?"

"When I help senior citizens cross the street, for instance, they sometimes send me gifts in the mail. My parents raised me to always reply with a thank-you card on such occasions."

Though Ida tossed it out there like it was nothing,

Midoriya was clearly impressed.

"That's kind of amazing, actually!"

"You think so? It seems perfectly ordinary."

Blushing at Midoriya's reaction, Ida glanced at Todoroki, hoping for backup.

"No. Can't say I've ever done that," came the blunt reply.

Ida slumped slightly and said, "Oh. I see..."

"B-but that's not a bad thing at all! Good experience, even, especially for an assignment like this!"

"Yes, of course! A letter is the perfect way to truly make one's feelings known. Which reminds me... Oh!"

Ida picked up a bit at Midoriya's reassurance and thrust both hands into the air.

"W-what's the matter, Ida?"

"How silly of me to forget!" said Ida, pulling an envelope out of his school bag.

"Forget what?"

"I received these theme park tickets from Native, for the three of us."

"Native? Who's that?" said Todoroki.

"The hero who was on the scene when we fought Stain!" answered Midoriya. "I wonder why, though?"

Ida removed four tickets from the envelope and said, "As a means of thanking us, I suspect."

"Why four?"

"Because most of the rides at theme parks are two-seaters? I guess Native was just trying to be considerate."

Todoroki nodded at Midoriya's guess.

"We ought to take advantage of his kindness and invite someone else to come along, no?"

"Good thinking!" said Midoriya, jumping at the idea.

Todoroki replied with "I guess so," which was more enthusiasm than they typically expected from him.

"However, these are only good through next week. Are the two of you free on Sunday?"

"Sunday...? Ack! Sorry, I can't make it!"

"Other plans, then?"

Midoriya's eyes grew wide and sparkled as he went on to explain, unable to contain his excitement.

"There's a hero exhibit at the culture hall! A can't-miss event covering everything from the dawn-of-heroes period! The stuff on display isn't usually available to the public, and everyone who attends gets a deluxe

photo collection with detailed profiles of those early heroes!"

"You sure are fond of heroes, Midoriya!"

"I'm really sorry!"

"I can't do Sunday either. Need to visit my mom. Sorry."

Ida responded to the apologies with a dejected "I see" but quickly snapped back to his usual driven self. "Unfortunate, yet unavoidable. I would hate for these tickets to go to waste, so I'll simply have to think of others to invite."

"The three of us'll have to go another time. Ah, I mean, if you guys want to, that is…"

Todoroki and Ida were baffled by Midoriya's sudden timid turn.

"Just saying… In case you two didn't actually want to go otherwise. Not trying to force it…"

At Midoriya's bashful explanation, his friends turned to each other for a moment.

"Midoriya. Though you possess that incredible strength, you hardly act like it!"

"It's true," said Todoroki, agreeing with the astounded Ida. Midoriya gave a weak chuckle and moved to change the subject.

"Um, anyhow, who's coming to Parents' Day from your family, Ida?"

"My mother," replied Ida sincerely. "My father has his work, you know. Will either of your folks be attending, Midoriya?"

"My mom, too. How about you, Todoroki…?"

"Me…? Probably no one."

Midoriya paused for a beat at his friend's nonchalant answer, uttered, "Oh," and turned pale. He was well aware of Todoroki's complicated home situation, so he instantly regretted raising the issue in the heat of the moment.

The number one hero was All Might, and the runner-up was Todoroki's father, Flame Hero: Endeavor. Though ambitious to a fault, Endeavor had never quite managed to rise above his rival, so he had chosen a different strategy. In order to create a powerful heir to inherit his fiery Quirk and then some, the man had singled out his would-be wife and forced her into a Quirk marriage designed to produce the ideal offspring. More than any of his siblings, young Todoroki had been blessed with a superior Quirk combining his father's fire powers and his mother's ice abilities. As he was

the one most likely to surpass All Might someday, the boy had endured brutal training under his father from an early age, and when his mother had tried to stick up for him, Endeavor had taken out his rage on her as well. Pushed to the psychological breaking point, Rei Todoroki had snapped one day and tossed scalding water on her own son, permanently scarring half of his face. She had been institutionalized ever since, giving Todoroki another reason to despise his father.

"Shoot. I'm sorry…"

"Ah, yes. Your mother is in the hospital. Apologies."

Todoroki brushed off his friends' earnest words and answered in his usual terse way.

"Don't worry about it. Nothing worth apologizing over."

"I'm certain your parents would be delighted to see how far you've come, though. It seems a shame," said Ida with a fervent nod. Todoroki reached into his pants pocket and felt the handout crumple in his hand.

"It's fine, really… Besides, last thing I want is that bastard showing up."

"Bastard? You mean Endeavor? You shouldn't call the man who raised you 'bastard.' Why not 'father,' at least?"

"Even 'bastard' is too good for my pathetic excuse of a father."

"If not 'father,' perhaps 'papa'?"

"Papa...?"

"Or 'daddy'?"

The mere thought of referring to Endeavor so affectionately brought a scowl to Todoroki's face, so Midoriya was quick to interject.

"H-hey, that's all right! There are plenty of families out there where kids call their parents by name, or by nicknames."

"But nicknames imply friendship among peers, no? It would seem disrespectful."

"A nickname? For that bastard...? Not a chance."

"Totally up to you what you call him, I say!" followed up Midoriya, realizing it was a lost cause. As they rounded the corner, Todoroki stopped.

"Todoroki?"

"Just remembered. I've got somewhere to be."

The boy's eyes seemed to wander as he spoke. Midoriya thought something must be up but decided to let it pass, waving goodbye to his friend instead.

"All right. See you tomorrow!"

"Farewell, Todoroki!"

"Sure."

ᴜᴀ

After splitting up with his classmates, Todoroki soon arrived at a large white building lit up in shades of orange by the setting sun. The hospital where his mother was institutionalized.

Though clinic hours were just about over, the lobby was brimming with patients waiting to check out. Todoroki glanced at the scene as he hurried into an elevator destined for the upper levels. It wasn't his first time coming here, but the boy noticed how nervous he was as he stared at the floor display, ticking up. Nothing could compare to that first visit, though. Back then, it wasn't until he saw his own hand trembling on the doorknob that he realized how unsettled he was about finally seeing his mother again.

The elevator doors slid open quietly, and Todoroki emerged into a corridor bathed in silence, unlike the lobby below. The faint scent of antiseptic common to most hospitals reminded him of his own recent stay; he and the other two had gotten hurt fighting Stain and had spent a few days convalescing in the aftermath.

Late one night, with Midoriya and Ida fast asleep, Todoroki's eyes had popped open, and in that cold, sterile silence, his mother had entered his thoughts. The still and the cold were nothing new to her. That had been her entire world for years, now.

"Shoto? What a nice surprise."

As he passed the nurses' station, a nurse he'd become acquainted with called out to Todoroki.

A "surprise"?

"Oh. Hi."

He had half a mind to ask a question, but the station phone started ringing, so he kept walking. The folded paper in his pocket seemed to grow heavier.

Arriving at his mother's room, Todoroki gave a short sigh and entered.

"Hi, Mom."

"Shoto?" said Rei Todoroki, turning to face him from the far side of the room. With the barred

window at her back, a soft smile crept into her eyes, which opened wide.

"What's wrong?"

"Oh… Nothing, honey. Come on in. Sit," replied his mother, offering Todoroki her own chair. He sat, and she stared at her son.

"Mom?" he asked, feeling awkward under her gaze, unsure what to make of it. She apologized with a sudden "Sorry" and slowly lowered herself onto the edge of the bed.

"It's fine… Is there something on my face, or…?"

"No. It's just… I haven't had the chance to see you on a school day in quite some time… You're growing up…"

His mother's eyes twinkled and narrowed, prompting an even more embarrassed Todoroki to cast his own eyes downward. He suddenly understood what the nurse had meant by "surprise"—this was his first-ever visit on a school day.

"Sorry for showing up unannounced."

"Don't be silly. I'm always happy to see you."

He somehow knew his mother would respond to the apology that way, and though her doting mostly made him uncomfortable, part of him embraced it. Being with his mother like this transported Todoroki back to his childhood, when he'd sworn that he'd save her from their tragic circumstances.

His fingertips brushed the handout in his pocket. Of course—the reason he'd come. His legs had carried him here, despite the fact that he knew full well she couldn't attend.

Was it even worth telling her?

Watching her taciturn son, Rei seemed to remember something and said, "Want anything to drink, honey?"

"Huh? Oh, sure."

Suddenly aware of how dry his throat was, he shot up, ready to run off and buy a drink or two.

"No need to leave. I have some things in the fridge," said his mother hurriedly, before he reached the door.

Todoroki checked the minifridge under the desk and found a few bottles of soft drinks, as well as a yogurt drink with a cartoon cow on the carton, clearly meant for children.

"Look, Shoto. Your old favorite—the yogurt with Mrs. Cow. I saw that they were selling it, so..."

Todoroki froze. He had a vague feeling that he'd

enjoyed the drink as a child but couldn't pinpoint a specific memory. His mother's broad grin changed to a sheepish smile upon noticing his reaction.

"But I know, I know. You're in high school now, so I picked out a few other options as well. Take whichever you'd like…"

He realized the trouble she'd gone to in anticipation of his visit, and it sent a pang through his heart.

"This one, I guess," he said, his hand reaching for Mrs. Cow without missing a beat. "Sure," replied his mother. The barely sweet drink seemed so familiar, though he still couldn't quite place it.

The hospital room grew quiet.

Todoroki finished his drink and began absent-mindedly fiddling with the empty carton. They could never reclaim the years they'd been apart, which now took the form of the silence flowing between mother and son. Still, the deliberate distance wasn't especially painful, and the measured silence was their considerate way of giving one another time to think.

"How's school?"

"Fine, I…"

For a brief moment Todoroki had felt at peace, until

he remembered the paper burning a hole in his pocket. It was now or never, but the more he thought about it, the more the words eluded him. His mother couldn't have known why he hesitated. Her face revealed her concern, prompting him to start talking about something—anything at all.

"We did rescue training in class today. Got to ride in a helicopter, even."

"A helicopter? Well, isn't that something," she said, showing genuine interest and mild surprise. Todoroki felt encouraged and went on.

"Because saving lives is a hero's job, after all."

"Mhm, that's right."

"We also slid down this evacuation chute."

"Oh?"

"And learned how to send out distress signals."

"I see."

"And then…"

His account of the day's events gushed forth, his mother beaming and nodding all the while.

"All Might was there too, teaching the class."

"You always were a fan of All Might, weren't you, Shoto? But you had to wait until your father wasn't

around to watch those video clips in secret. Remember?"

"Uh-huh…"

All Might had been the sort of hero Todoroki admired as a child, but along the way, he'd shut away those feelings so deep inside that he'd mostly forgotten. He recalled the pair of bloodied, misshapen hands that had reminded him, and said to his mother, "There's this guy. Midoriya."

"Someone in your class?"

"Yeah."

Back when they'd started high school, Todoroki had barely been aware of Midoriya. The latter was oddly timid, but now and then he'd blow everyone away with his power and gusto during class—especially when the League of Villains attacked U.S.J. Todoroki came to realize that All Might had taken an interest in Midoriya, so the son of Endeavor had made a point of throwing down the gauntlet at the Sports Festival.

With burning hatred for his father, Todoroki had set out to beat Midoriya without using his fiery left side—the half of him his mother implicitly feared and rejected. That would've been revenge enough, and he'd relished the dumbfounded look on his father's face during the battle against his classmate. Nonetheless, Midoriya had kept fighting with all his might and zero regard for his mangled body, raging against Todoroki for thinking he could win with only half his innate strength.

"Your power is your own!" his opponent had shouted, and the words had penetrated Todoroki. Midoriya—crippled beyond belief yet still obnoxiously powerful and giving it his all—had been the one to get through to him, pushing ever forward like the heroes Todoroki had once admired.

Midoriya's white-hot passion translated not into words but rather a sort of nostalgia for Todoroki's long since abandoned fire. In the moment, it had helped Todoroki forget everything—including his hatred for his father—and in doing so, he realized he'd been shackling himself.

"We fought. At the Sports Festival. He was all beat-up and his hands were practically falling off, but he just kept coming at me."

"Oh my!"

"So I had to use my full power against him. For the first time ever."

"Did you, now?"

"He's something special."

His mother smiled softly at him.

"It sounds like you've made quite the friend."

Seeing her beaming eyes tear up a bit, Todoroki slowly nodded.

"Yeah."

Another moment of silence. A gentle silence, though, that made Todoroki feel bashful in spite of himself.

"Mom, I've got your laundry and... Oh. Shoto? This is a surprise. What's going on?"

The boy's older sister, Fuyumi Todoroki, broke the silence as she entered her mother's room. The two women resembled each other in some ways, but Fuyumi came off brighter and cheerier than her somewhat faded mother.

"'Surprise'? That's twice, now..."

"Twice what?"

"Nothing. Forget it."

"Hmm? Oh. Mom. I'm leaving your laundry here, okay?"

"Thanks as always, honey."

"Don't mention it."

As if she'd done it a million times before, Fuyumi stuffed the bundle of clothing onto a shelf.

"Any special reason you're here today?" she asked her little brother.

"Not really."

Just as Todoroki stood up to throw away the empty drink carton, the crucial handout fell from his pocket to the floor.

"Hmm? What's this?"

"No... Don't..." said Todoroki, but Fuyumi had already turned to pick up and unfold the paper.

"A notice about Parents' Day?"

"Oh...?"

"None of your business."

"Right, right. I get what's going on."

Fuyumi had figured it out, just like that, and her brother instinctively returned her smile with a scowl, frustrated over all the time he'd spent in angst, and for what? His mother's voice snapped him out of it.

"Shoto... I'm sorry. I'm afraid I can't attend..."

He didn't know what to do with the heartfelt apology.

"No, I, uh, just wanted to pass on the notice... No big deal, really..."

Regretting everything, Todoroki wished she'd never found out. He wished he'd never come. Not if she felt forced to apologize over it.

"I'm sorry, Mom…"

"Oh, Shoto…"

Rei's face crumpled at her son's own small apology.

"H-hey, c'mon, now…" interjected Fuyumi, in a slight panic over the unintentional role she'd played. But then her face lit up, as if in a eureka moment.

"I know! I can attend Parents' Day!"

"Huh? That's crazy. And you've got your own school to worry about," shot back Shoto, referring to the elementary school where his sister taught.

"Nice of you to worry, but I can put in for half a day off since this is a family affair. Plus, I can record the whole thing!"

Todoroki was aghast at what his grinning sister clearly thought was a brilliant idea.

"This isn't like Sports Day with the little kids you teach."

"Oh? Don't want me to? I'm telling you, though, there are plenty of camcorders in the room when my kids have Parents' Day."

"Why not, then…?" said their mother, before Todoroki could tell his sister off for comparing him, a high schooler, to her ankle biters. Apparently Rei had been delighted with Fuyumi's idea, as her beaming face had clouded over when her son protested. Todoroki was at a loss for words. He hated this plan, but he couldn't very well break his mother's heart.

"I'd have to check with my school…"

A strained concession through gritted teeth. It was nearly dinnertime, so Todoroki and Fuyumi left the room and started down the corridor.

"Your homeroom teacher is…Aizawa, right?"

"Yeah…"

"What's the matter, Mister Grumpy? Oh, I know… Why not have Dad attend instead?"

"Don't you breathe a word to him."

"But…"

"Just. Don't."

Fuyumi's face twisted in grief for her bullheaded brother, but it didn't take long for her usual smile to return.

"Oh, fine."

While waiting for the elevator, she noticed just how grim and forlorn Todoroki was looking.

"You hate the camcorder idea that much? Would

anything convince you?"

"Yeah, I hate it, but it's more than that," replied her brother, lifting his head.

"What, then?"

"I knew all along she couldn't go, so she never should've had to find out in the first place."

"Ah. That," said Fuyumi with an easy smile, bopping Todoroki on the head.

"What the hell?"

"Listen. There's no parent out there who wouldn't be thrilled to learn their child actually thinks about them. Mom might feel terrible about not being able to go, but I know she was glad you came to tell her anyway. Remember, it's not just your first Parents' Day notice. In a way, it's hers, too."

Todoroki saw the wisdom in his sister's words. "You ought to be a teacher or something."

"You don't say?"

Todoroki tried to hide his embarrassment, but his sister gave him another bop on the head anyway. The elevator announced its arrival with a ding. The doors opened.

"Shoto? Better get in, or I'm leaving you behind," said Fuyumi, prompting Todoroki to hop over the threshold. His sister, there on the day of? With a camcorder? Mortifying, to be sure, but a small price to pay to make his mother happy.

Shota Aizawa made a point of living his life rationally. In other words, cutting out all that was unnecessary, extraneous, or wasteful. Accordingly, he had no preferences when it came to food or clothing, because time spent fussing over such things was time wasted. His hair was long and unkempt, and his outfits were all identical or, at the very least, indistinguishable from one another. In his eyes, the only point of eating was to nourish oneself, so he mostly subsisted on nutrient jelly. Clothing and living spaces that emphasized form over function and comfort were absurd to him; cooking elaborate meals and caring where the ingredients were grown or processed was nonsensical.

Unfortunately for Aizawa, the world was full of the extraneous.

"Hello? This is your son's homeroom teacher, Aizawa. Do you have a moment? No, Fumikage isn't in any trouble. I'm actually calling about the Parents' Day we're holding next week... Yes. There's something I'd like to discuss."

It was after school in the staff room. As inimitable as the great U.A. was in many respects, the staff room made it look like any other high school. The teachers' desks were grouped by class year and department, and the shelves lining one wall were stuffed with files and books on education. The one thing that set U.A. apart was its faculty, every member of which was a professional hero.

While Aizawa gave Fumikage Tokoyami's family a summary of the event to come, sitting on his left was the R-Rated Hero: Midnight, who fiddled with her trademark weapon, a whip. She seemed to be wearing nothing but bondage gear that revealed every curve and contour, but underneath that was in fact an ultrathin bodysuit. Midnight's titillating appearance routinely flustered male students with even the remotest interest in the opposite sex, while lust-crazed imps like Minoru Mineta did nothing to hide the way their teacher made them feel.

Across from Midnight sat the bulky, angular Cementoss. Busy preparing the next day's lesson plan for his contemporary literature class, he was showing a textbook to and asking advice from his colleague, Thirteen, a teacher dressed in a spacesuit. To the side, Ectoplasm enjoyed a break with a cup of tea, which the eerie, pitch-black teacher sipped through his large white teeth. These heroes in full costume would hardly come off as educators at a glance, but this was an everyday scene in the staff room at U.A. High.

Incidentally, class 1-B's homeroom teacher, Vlad King, was patrolling the school grounds, Snipe was overseeing the marksmanship club, Power Loader was helping Support Course students test their inventions, and Present Mic was away from his desk, in the bathroom.

"...looking forward to your cooperation next week. Goodbye, then."

Aizawa ended the call and stared at the paper in

front of him—a list of his students' names and contact info, with check marks next to those whose families he'd already reached out to. He checked off Tokoyami.

Next is Todoroki.

But nobody at the Todoroki household was picking up. Not home, perhaps. Aizawa waited a few rings before hanging up and checking Todoroki's emergency contact—a cell phone number belonging to the boy's father, the hero Endeavor. For all Aizawa knew, Endeavor could be on the job, but as 1-A's homeroom teacher considered his options, a voice spoke to him from behind.

"Something wrong, Aizawa?"

It was All Might in his true form. Instead of the trademark solid frame and explosive muscles, there stood a gaunt man who was nothing but skin and bones, with deep, dark circles around his sunken eye sockets.

"No... I just couldn't get ahold of anyone at Todoroki's house."

"Young Todoroki, huh... Did you try his emergency contact?"

"Not yet. You-know-who might be working."

All Might glanced at Aizawa's list.

"Endeavor, right! Why don't you let me handle this one?"

"Eh?"

"I've been wanting to talk to the man ever since the Sports Festival, actually!"

With a grunt, All Might bulked up into his muscle form, the sudden transformation knocking away his chair. He plucked it off the ground as if it were doll furniture, returned to his desk, and started dialing the phone.

"Let's see… Zero, nine… Ah, wrong button! These giant fingers sure weren't made for dialing."

"Why transform at all, then?"

"Because my voice changes too, and I need him to recognize me! Zero, nine… Ack."

All Might's sausage fingers had failed him once again, which irked Aizawa enough that he leaped from his seat and dialed the number himself. Nothing grated on his nerves like wasted time.

Blithely unaware of his colleague's internal rage, All Might grinned and said, "Thank you, Aizawa! You're nicer than people give you credit for!"

People? Which people…?

The backhanded compliment weighed on Aizawa's mind for a moment, but he soon returned to his rational center and his list.

Bakugo next…

He picked up the receiver and was about to dial when All Might's voice boomed.

"Ah, is that you, Endeavor? It's me, All Might!"

What, they're pals now?

All Might's easygoing tone triggered Aizawa's internal snark.

"Heyyy, how've you been? Shame we had so little time to chat at the Sports Festival, am I right? Anyway, we oughta sit down for tea one of these days and… Huh? 'Leave your message after the tone'…? Drat, voice mail!"

Slow on the uptake, aren't you?

All Might's airheaded move distracted Aizawa enough that he misdialed.

"Kinda nervous, having to leave a message… Hrm."

All Might cleared his throat as if preparing a formal speech.

"Hey, Endeavor! Guess who?"

Why the pointless quiz?

The increasingly irritated Aizawa wasn't trying to eavesdrop, but it was hard not to.

"The answer is...All Might! Anyway, we haven't talked since the Sports Festival, but I'm hoping we get a chance to catch up soon! About how to raise this next generation, and the like. In fact, I found this great vintage café that brews a mean cup of coffee! You're a java man, right? You mentioned that to me...about ten years ago, I think? Something about the perfect beans? To be honest, I'm the sort of lowbrow who'd settle for canned coffee! Oh. Ran out of time."

"All Might. What was the point of that?"

"Eh, the point...? Ah, so sorry! Parents' Day, right! Let me try again..."

"Never mind. I'll just send a fax straight to Endeavor's agency."

Calling again would be a waste of time, and another attempt at a message? Forget it. Realizing he should've handled it this way from the start, Aizawa took the Parents' Day handout over to the fax machine.

"Sorry, Aizawa... Urk!"

True to form, blood gushed from All Might's mouth as he reverted to his true form.

"Wow! Two seconds I'm back from the toilet, and already there's blood!" shouted Present Mic with all his usual enthusiasm. The sunglasses, the trimmed mustache, the hair slicked straight up into the air—all of it utterly extraneous, in Aizawa's eyes.

"You okay, All Might? Looks like you need some liver in your diet! And, oh—the principal wants to see you in his office."

"I wonder why... Hopefully not more of his elaborate educational theories."

All Might slunk off—clearly not crazy about what was sure to be another long lecture—and Midnight cheered him on with a half-hearted "Good luck." Heroes or not, the teachers were still civil servants at the beck and call of their superiors.

"Oh, faxing something? Wonder when that's gonna fall out of style!"

Mic's attention had shifted to Aizawa, whom he now closed in on. The former was like a bad cold the latter just couldn't shake, going back as far as their days as classmates at U.A. Mic glanced at his colleague's fax.

"Ahh, contacting the parents, huh. Homeroom teachers have got it rough."

"I suppose so."

Despite his answer, Aizawa didn't actually think it was all that rough. Reaching out to the families like this was a necessary part of the job, after all, but going out of his way to explain that to Mic would've crossed the line into irrational territory. None the wiser that Aizawa had intentionally tried to cut the conversation short, Mic went on and suddenly seemed to remember something.

"Hey, hey, how's that thing coming along?"

"What thing?"

"The big hostage situation thing!"

"Oh. That. Well, we've…"

Without waiting for Aizawa to finish, Mic puffed out his chest and shouted.

"I've come up with a real hot idea! Somebody stop me, I'm so clever! Hey! Teachers! Wanna hear my frosty-cool plan? Everybody say 'yeahhh'!"

But instead of the resounding "yeahhh" Mic sought from the Hero Course faculty, all he got was a "Sure, sure, what now?" from a visibly annoyed Midnight.

"I know this crowd can do better than that!"

"Don't count on it."

Midnight raised her hand with as little enthusiasm as possible.

"How about the nosebleed seats?"

"Oh. Does he mean us?" asked Cementoss, now paying attention.

"I would prefer silence."

"Aw, let's hear him out, at least."

Thirteen tried convincing Ectoplasm to put down his tea and play along, while Mic continued.

"First! Holding a big group hostage means you gotta make 'em stay put, right? And my Voice is the perfect tool for the job!"

"This is what you were getting at...?"

But Aizawa's hushed exasperation was drowned out by Mic's bloviating. Present Mic's Quirk, "Voice," gave his voice a range from soprano to bass and made it loud enough to be wielded as a weapon.

"I'd gather those hostages behind closed doors and give 'em a front-row seat to my explosive live show! It'd break their hearts and their eardrums, knocking 'em out cold! Any hardheaded heroes who came along to save the day would also get brought to their knees by my sweet voice! Go, go, heaven! A foolproof plan,

wouldn'tcha say? Well?"

"No. Listen here..." Aizawa started to say to the smug Mic, but this time he was cut off by Midnight's languid dissent.

"Eh? I say you're just too loud. It's enough to make a gal lose interest in a hurry."

"Huhh? What's wrong with being loud?"

"Personally, I prefer it when someone holds back in silence until it all comes leaking out in a nice moan."

"Midnight, do try to contain yourself," said Thirteen, who was likely blushing under his costume's helmet.

"Such a prude, Thirteen. All I mean is that it ought to be done smarter, not louder."

"You have a point, I suppose," said Cementoss, but Mic wasn't having it.

"What's wrong with my plan? This is one listener who's dying to know!"

"Knocking them out cold is all well and good, until they regain consciousness."

"In that case, I'd just keep the noise coming with an all-night live show!"

"That's not all, though. Bursting their eardrums,

really? No. With my Quirk, I could keep the hostages in place and even send their would-be rescuers to dreamland."

Midnight's Quirk was "Somnambulist," and it allowed her to release a soporific scent into the air—an effect said to work better on men than on women.

"Nice and peaceful, and nobody needs to get hurt."

But Ectoplasm raised his head and took issue with Midnight's approach.

"Peaceful…? Seems unnecessary, given what we're discussing. Because taking hostages still counts as a crime, and whoever heard of a peaceful crime?"

"But we wouldn't want to actually hurt anyone!"

"Naive, Thirteen. However, my clones are the perfect solution in this case, as I could have them stand guard. One clone for each hostage."

Ectoplasm's Quirk was "Clones." He could spew an ectoplasm-like substance from his mouth, and, at will, have it transform into copies of himself. Typically his limit was thirty clones at once, but that number would shoot up to thirty-six after two or three songs at karaoke, once his jaw could open wider.

"Actually, I don't think…"

But Aizawa went unheard.

"Hmph. What if one of the hostages had a strong Quirk and just blasted past your clones? My putting them all to sleep still seems like the strongest option."

At this, Cementoss's beady eyes glinted.

"Strongest? I'm afraid I can't agree there."

"And why not, Cementoss?"

"In our world, you can't toss that word around unless you're talking about All Might."

"C'mon…"

"He could round up the hostages and bind them in an instant. Not to mention, he'd blow away any and all heroes trying to save them."

"Yikes, you're right! The strongest hero would make for the strongest villain!"

As the teachers yapped and imagined All Might's turn to the dark side, Aizawa still couldn't get a word in edgewise.

Annoying…

He decided to forget about his gregarious colleagues for a second and get back to the task at hand. Although Aizawa was no stranger to reining in unruly students when they dared interrupt his lessons, he knew that unruly coworkers were best ignored.

"Hello? This is Katsuki's homeroom teacher, Aizawa. Do you have a moment?"

The others left Aizawa to his calls, and the debate raged on.

"Sure, All Might is the strongest. I'll give you that. But how would you go about it, Cementoss? You'd surround the hostages with cement, right?"

Cementoss's Quirk was "Cement," and he could manipulate cement with a mere touch as if it were modeling clay. He paused for a moment before answering.

"Surround them? No. I'd cover the whole group with a cement dome, and any heroes would get the same treatment. Nowhere to run for hostages and heroes alike."

Cementoss gave a satisfied nod, but his suggestion didn't sit well with Thirteen.

"Um, wouldn't everyone end up suffocating, though…?"

"So be it. The important thing is that the hostages can't escape."

"I concur," said Ectoplasm, chiming in.

"Ehh? Surely that's going too far…" shot back the flustered Thirteen just as Present Mic's hands came

down on his shoulders from above.

"Lighten up, Wet Blanket Boy!"

"'Boy'...? I-I'm twenty-eight years old, I'll have you know."

"Wet Blanket Man, then! And we still haven't heard from you."

"Me? Right... I suppose I would use my Black Hole...?"

The black holes produced by Thirteen's Quirk could suck in matter and obliterate it down to the atomic level.

"Now who's 'going too far'?"

"Atomizing the hostages would defeat the purpose of having hostages in the first place," said Ectoplasm.

"Wow! Thirteen seems so harmless, but he's got the blackest heart of all! Hoo boy!" Mic chimed in.

"Mmm, I have to admit, I'm a fan of that devilish discrepancy," said Midnight.

"No, no, that's not what I meant!"

About to finish his call, Aizawa was still half listening.

"...we'll see you next week. Goodbye."

Next up is Hagakure...

Before he could pick up the receiver and dial the

next number, the phone rang.

"Hello? You've reached U.A. High School."

"Hi, I'm calling about Shoto Todoroki, in class 1-A. Could you get me Aizawa, his homeroom teacher?"

Aizawa ran through Todoroki's family members in his mind, trying to figure out who the young-sounding, feminine voice belonged to.

Todoroki… In his family, he's got…

"Yes, this is Aizawa. Whom do I have the pleasure of speaking with…?"

"Ah, sorry! I'm Shoto's older sister, Fuyumi Todoroki. And thanks for all you do for him."

"Perfect. I was trying to reach your household, actually."

"Really? I'm just on my way home now. Staff meeting ran a little late…"

Aizawa's eyes opened a little wider at the all-too-familiar phrase.

"Staff meeting? Oh, you teach elementary, right?"

"Ah, yeah. Something a little funny about this, talking teacher to teacher."

Unlike Todoroki, his older sister had no trouble

keeping a conversation going.

Guess she wouldn't make a very good schoolteacher if she were as surly as him.

"Um, so...is everything okay with Shoto...?"

A note of concern entered her voice as she realized that Aizawa must have wanted to get in touch for a reason.

"Everything's just fine. I'm making calls about Parents' Day."

"Oh, of course."

Aizawa was quick to get to the point, and the relief in her voice was palpable. He recalled his early impressions of Todoroki at the start of the school year. The boy's talents had been obvious, but he hadn't exactly played well with others. In elementary school, his behavior had probably triggered a number of troubling calls to the Todoroki home.

"May I ask who will be attending Parents' Day next week?"

"Ah, that would be me. That's actually what I'm calling about..."

"How can I help?"

"Would it be all right if I brought a camcorder to the

event? I'd be sure to keep out of the way, of course."

A camcorder? For home videos, to commemorate the occasion?

Aizawa tilted his head, thinking about the unusual request.

"I'm sorry, but for security reasons, we don't allow recording devices on campus."

"Right. I understand…"

He could practically hear the disappointment in her voice, but her chipper tone returned after he briefly explained the reasoning behind the rule.

"We'll see you next week, then. Goodbye."

"Sounds good. Thanks again."

As Aizawa ended the call and checked another name off the list, a thought occurred to him.

What if it wasn't just to mark the occasion, but instead to…

Present Mic's bombastic voice came crashing into Aizawa's ears.

"Well, I'd just jack into the broadcast station and send my sound waves soaring, on air! With everyone knocked out, I'd nab the jewels and the damsel's heart! Like a regular Lupin III!"

"Jewel thievery's not as easy as cartoons make it out to be. Those jewelry stores have tight security, you know?"

"My voice breaks ladies' hearts and reinforced glass into a million pieces!"

"Who wants to know about the bad things I'd do? Just kneel down and lick my boots if you want to hear."

"I'll pass on that."

Midnight's bewitching smile had no effect on Cementoss, whose rejection was as blunt as his square body.

"You too, Cementoss? Such a stick-in-the-mud. Fine. I'll tell you all, no charge. I'd put a person to sleep and figure out their weaknesses—for blackmail."

"How deceitful," said Ectoplasm.

"A bit mundane, but realistic enough, in a bad way," said Thirteen, shaking his head dismissively.

"But what if they had no secrets to exploit?"

"In that case...I'd frame them somehow. Work a little magic while they slept, if you know what I mean," answered Midnight, shooting Cementoss a buttery-smooth wink.

"How underhanded," said Ectoplasm.

"So believable it's scary," said Thirteen.

"Bad and sexy...? That makes you the Fujiko to my Lupin!"

While Aizawa had been on the phone, it seemed that the teachers' conversation had turned to boasts about what sort of wicked things they might do with their Quirks.

These people, I swear...

Tossing out a retort would only drag him down to their level, though. Eager to be done with his list, Aizawa soothed his dry eyes with some eye drops, pulled himself together, and picked up the receiver once more.

"I wonder why talking about doing bad gets me so hot and bothered? I'm aching inside, just thinking about it."

"Such is human nature."

"But we're heroes. It's just not right."

"C'mon, Thirteen! It's just hypothetical! Pure, 100 percent fantasy!" said Mic, slapping Thirteen on the shoulder playfully. Meanwhile, Cementoss seemed interested in exploring Midnight's question.

"Come to think of it, we all wanted to become he-

roes from a young age, no? Which meant internalizing the idea that we mustn't ever do wrong. Suppressing that side of ourselves."

"Self-denial makes that eventual gratification all the spicier, but one mustn't let it build up too much. Everyone needs a good release now and then. It'd be simple enough, boys—just say the word. Toss away the pride that's holding you back, and I'd be happy to make you my house pets."

"I'll pass on that too," said Cementoss with a flat chuckle.

"This sort of thought experiment isn't entirely without merit, though. It could even help us understand the mind of a villain," mused Ectoplasm.

"That's true enough," said Thirteen.

"Right, exactly!" blurted out Mic. "Speaking of a good 'release,' everyone's used their Quirk to play a prank or two when they were kids, yeah? This is just like that!"

Thirteen shook his head and said, "Pranks? Not me."

Seriously?

In the middle of a phone call once again, Aizawa overheard his colleagues' conversation and wondered to himself about Thirteen. Mic couldn't believe it either, and he wasn't shy about it.

"Seriously?! Never? Not once in your life? Glory be, we're in the presence of Saint Thirteen!"

We're on the same page for once? Really?

"Oh. Pardon me. Right, so on the day of..." continued Aizawa with a scowl.

"I don't suppose you'd tell us what sort of pranks you committed, Present Mic?"

Mic thought about Thirteen's question and answered proudly.

"When my friend was snoozing at lunchtime, sometimes I'd start spitting rhymes right into his ear!"

"Such a rude awakening would be enough to stop my heart, I daresay."

"Other times, I'd interrupt his naps with drawn-out, immersive ghost stories!"

"Your poor friend."

Unable to let it slide, Aizawa placed his hand over the receiver and muttered, "That friend was me, by the way."

"Ohh, true enough, old buddy, old pal! Sorry, sorry! But what say we flush that ancient history down

the toilet?"

"An appropriate solution for all your bullcrap."

Wishing he could flush the memories, too, Aizawa tuned out his old classmate's blathering and sympathetic look before returning to the phone call.

"Mrs. Midoriya? Sorry about that… Now, as I was saying…"

Meanwhile, Present Mic had already flushed away whatever guilt he might've been feeling.

"Let's hear about your pranks, Midnight! Guessing you were always R-rated, even as a kid?"

"No dirty stories, please," begged Ectoplasm.

"Not at all—I was a charming little girl. But…there was that time my first crush and I played doctor."

"Ooh. Any stethoscopes involved? Listening to each other all over?"

An excited Present Mic had taken the bait, but Midnight flashed a beguiling smile and said, "I'll leave that to your imaginations. Let's just say it escalated until we went from playing doctor to playing surgeon…"

"Eh. What kind of surgery…?"

The expressions of Midnight's male colleagues grew rigid.

"Heh heh. Like I said, imagination. In any case, that

boy went on to bat for the other team, and I might've played a role…"

"W-what'd you do to the guy?" cried Mic, hands guarding his own nether regions. Another chuckle escaped Midnight's lips as she reminisced.

"It all must've been a little too stimulating for him…"

"Doesn't sound like that should be a fond memory for you! Back me up, Thirteen?"

"Well, to start with, that bit of mischief had nothing to do with her Quirk."

"I suppose it didn't. Whatever. Let's hear some more stories—how about you, Ectoplasm?" said Midnight, egging on her colleague.

"Though I have never used my Quirk in service of a prank, there was one time when I acted in error…"

Ectoplasm's solemn tone made his pro hero colleagues all the more eager to hear.

"Confessing to a crime, huh? This oughta be great! Go on and paint for us a real clear picture of what went down!"

"But you're so very stoic, Ectoplasm. I can hardly imagine you committing a wrongdoing."

"Alas, a sin is a sin… I exercise my right to remain silent."

"Teasing us like that just makes it worse, y'know."

"It's true! Now we want to hear!"

True to his word, Ectoplasm remained silent.

"Hey, hey, you can't do that to us! Better not leave your audience hanging!"

"I only wish the memories could be purged."

Given his busybody coworkers, Ectoplasm was suddenly regretting piping up at all when Cementoss decided to speak. "Confession is good for the soul. And as your colleagues, we'd be happy to help lighten the burden you've been carrying."

Genuine compassion glinted in Cementoss's tiny eyes, touching Ectoplasm's heart.

"Well, this was back when I was in grade school..."

Present Mic and the others sat with bated breath, eager to hear the story.

Didn't take much to make him sing.

"Ah, hello. Is this the Mineta household? I'm Minoru's homeroom teacher, Aizawa, and... Yes. Of course. We appreciate all you do, too. I'm actually calling about Parents' Day..."

The voice inside Aizawa's head spouted its usual, rational snark as he continued down his call list, which was nearly finished. Not that the heavyhearted Ectoplasm was any the wiser.

"One morning, I found myself unable to extricate myself from the comfort of my bedchamber, and time itself seemed to elapse at the speed of light..."

"Huh? I don't get it," said Present Mic with a tilt of his head.

"He overslept," explained Cementoss.

"Though gripped by despair, I dashed to the schoolhouse, undeterred... Alas, the merciless morning bell rang out before I could enter, so I sent one of my clones into the classroom instead..."

"Meaning, you used a clone to avoid being marked late to school?"

"Indeed. My perfect attendance award was at stake, though I know now that no such excuse can make up for my grave sin..."

The surrounding heroes blinked at each other and let loose with disappointed sighs.

"That's all? You used your wits to solve the problem and still walked away with perfect attendance?"

"We were expecting a lot more from your 'sin.' Like a Shakespearean tragedy, full of love and deceit."

"The fault is with you people for expecting more. I only spoke my truth," shot back Ectoplasm. He went on to sip his tea, visibly grumpy with the others' reactions. Suddenly, Thirteen was reminded of a story of his own.

"I have an embarrassing tale as well. Once, I wet the bed and destroyed the evidence by sucking the very futon into one of my black holes..."

"Now that's using your noggin. Wish I'd had that option, way back!"

"But I got in trouble for it all the same," confessed Thirteen, scratching his helmet sheepishly.

"Bed-wetting? That's kinda cute, coming from you."

"How about you then, Cementoss? Did you ever get up to any mischief?"

"Me? Right... I once put up a wall of cement to avoid being caught in hide-and-seek. That's the worst I'm willing to admit."

The heroes pounced on Cementoss's flat smile.

"So there are things you won't cop to...?"

"Better to let sleeping dogs lie! Like my gramps always said, the scariest people are the ones you'd never expect!"

"This, after I was forced to confess? How cowardly."

"I'm dying to hear this, too. Especially now that we know it's such a secret."

Thirteen and Mic were content to leave Cementoss's dark past buried, while Ectoplasm and Midnight wanted it all dragged out into the light.

"Please, I was only joking," said Cementoss with a laugh.

"What? A joke? Don't scare us like that."

"Jokes are meant to be funny."

"Your sense of humor ain't doing my blood pressure any favors, Cementoss!"

"I'm sorry, really. And my best regards to your wise grandfather, Mic."

"Yeah, well, we won't forget this."

"Flush it all down the toilet, I say!"

He'll need to call a plumber, at this rate.

"…and we're looking forward to seeing you next week."

Aizawa hung up the phone and checked off "Yaoyorozu"—the final name on his list. He sighed, glad to be done with the mundane yet exhausting task. Meanwhile, his coworkers continued yapping, oblivious to his minor accomplishment, and he eyed them in amazement.

How long can five people talk about nothing whatso-ever...?

"With all our Quirks combined, we'd make for one nasty villain team! The world'd be no match for us!" shouted Present Mic, his boast filling the room.

U̲A̲

"Well, aren't you all in high spirits?"

"Sir!"

Principal Nezu had emerged from his office with All Might in tow. He was plainly a mouse, though in certain lighting he could resemble a dog, or even a small bear. Whatever he was, the adorable animal was dressed in a sharp suit vest and oversized shoes, and he rose only to All Might's knee.

"Did I hear something about you all taking on the world?"

The cute facade was, in the end, just a facade, for Nezu's scarred right eye held a certain intensity and hinted at a dark past. At the principal's implicit reproach, the teachers scrambled to explain themselves.

"No, it's not what you think! We were just discuss -ing how to handle you-know-what!"

"Exactly. Just brainstorming which of our Quirks could best handle a group of hostages, and so on."

"Ah, yes. I do know what," said Nezu with a nod.

"How would you go about it, sir?"

Nezu scratched his chin, ruminating on Midnight's question.

"First, I would prepare a giant maze."

"A maze, sir? Why go that route...?"

"Why? Hostages are taken for a reason, of course. The hostage taker may do it to evade capture, to acquire some reward, or simply to garner attention... If I were a villain, however, my hostages would be in service of an experiment."

"An experiment?"

"Indeed! I would place them at the maze's center, forcing their would-be rescuers to navigate the labyrinth under a time limit. Mind you, there would be electric fences, pitfalls, shifting walls...all to provide a proper challenge. Perhaps even doors that would require the heroes to solve complex puzzles to open..."

Principal Nezu's Quirk was "High Specs," making

him an exceedingly rare example of an intelligent animal with a superpower. Truly a unique individual.

"And any paths trodden would be sealed off, just as life offers no second chances… Heh heh… Ha ha ha ha! I wonder how many clever little mice would reach the goal in time…?"

Nezu's cackle offered an unsettling glimpse at the grudge he bore for the humans who'd once toyed with his life, which put a damper on the teachers' earlier excitement.

"Whoa, that's more than just blackhearted. We're talking a double shot of espresso, hold the cream!"

"Sir, I think you're scaring everyone," said All Might, crouching low to face his boss.

Nezu seemed to come to his senses.

"Oh my, I lost myself for a moment, there. In any case, heroes must always overcome the high walls they face and engender that Plus Ultra spirit! In that sense, my maze would provide the ideal trial! Oh. Leaving already, Aizawa?"

The unkempt teacher had put his desk in order and now stood.

"Yes. I'm finished for today."

"Like hell you are. You still gotta tell us how you'd wrangle a bunch of hostages. Admit it—my Quirk would be super handy!"

"As I said, I could just put them to sleep. My Quirk is best suited to the task."

"No, mine."

"Remember, everyone—safety should be our number one concern."

"I think we ought to team up to get the job done, no?"

"You said it!"

As the others agreed with Cementoss, a puzzled All Might cocked his head.

"Hmm? Isn't everything already set for you-know-what, Aizawa?"

"Yes. It is."

All Might aside, the other heroes gasped at Aizawa's deadpan declaration.

"For real? Why didn't you say something sooner?"

"You started running your mouths before I had a chance to. Anyhow, I'm leaving," grumbled Aizawa, glancing at the windows and realizing how dark it had gotten.

"After all our brainstorming?" came the first of a

flurry of complaints, but he was already moving towards the door.

Reminds me of the kids just before class begins.

There was nothing rational about getting worked up over nonsense, like a bunch of adolescents. Or about wasting valuable time and energy on heated conversations over nothing. Though Aizawa would lay down the law of rationality to keep classes running smoothly, he wasn't so high-handed as to impose his mantra on the students during their free time. After all, forcing one's beliefs on others like that would be in itself irrational.

What makes it so fun for them, exactly?

The kids would work themselves into a frenzy, chatting about whatever. Or lose heart over the smallest things. Or explode over differing opinions. No, nothing rational about youth—that point in life when one would dash headlong toward truth only to ignore it when it presented itself. Finding a satisfying answer to life's problems would inevitably involve quite a bit of wasted time and effort, so reducing that waste was key if one ever wanted to arrive at a conclusion.

His students' faces floated across Aizawa's mind. So

young and foolish. So full of potential but also wasted effort.

People worth teaching…

Hidden underneath the bandage-like wrapping that served as his weapon, Aizawa's mouth curled into a smile so faint the man himself didn't realize. The world was full of the extraneous, but at the very least, Aizawa would do his part to stay rational.

Part 4
Theme Park Panic

"Which looks better, Izuku?"

Sunday morning. Ready to head out to his long-awaited hero exhibit, Midoriya found himself confronted by a pair of skirt suits—one navy blue, one pale pink. His indecisive mother brought each one up to her body, back and forth.

"Going somewhere special?" he asked. The concern left Inko Midoriya's face as she lit up.

"Not now—this is for Parents' Day tomorrow. Well? Which one?"

Her expression grew deadly serious again, and Midoriya could only laugh, unsure how to respond. Nothing he'd learned at U.A. had prepared the high schooler to give fashion advice, but he couldn't very well blow her off with an evasive "Whichever." He thought for a moment and somehow settled on navy.

"That one...?"

"Navy? Isn't it a little dark?"

"The other one, then?"

"But then people might think I'm not dressing my age? Are you sure?"

"It'll be fine, probably. Anyway, I really gotta run..."

"Pink it is, then..." said his mother, moving towards the laundry room to check out the chosen skirt suit in the mirror. Midoriya seized his chance and made for the door.

"Wait. I think the pink makes me look fatter than I am...?"

His full-figured mother's trip to the mirror must've triggered her insecurities, because she scampered over to Midoriya, who'd only made it as far as the entryway.

"If you're that worried, navy works too," he said, stuffing his feet into his oversized shoes. Inko kept glancing between the two options.

"Right. Besides, navy hides stains better."

"Stains?" said Midoriya, and as he turned, he

noticed his mother's mouth gasp and clamp shut, as if she'd said too much. Puzzled, he tilted his head.

"Did the pink one get dirty or something?"

"Ah, that's not it! I mean… We're going to tour the facilities, right? Like that U.S.J. disaster dome? I'd better be prepared to pick up a little grime in hectic places like that," she said with an awkward smile. "Anyhow, you're taking off somewhere?"

"Oh. Yeah."

"What about lunch?"

"I'll pick up something while I'm out, but I'll be home by dinner!"

"Be safe out there, Izuku."

With his mother's send-off, Midoriya stepped out the front door at a brisk pace and hurtled down the stairs leading from the top floor of their garden-variety apartment complex. His mother sure had been acting odd, but the nagging thought soon floated off, like the thin clouds in the fair skies above. Grinning all the while, he set out on his usual route to the train station through a neighborhood that countryfolk might view as urban but that city dwellers would think downright provincial.

Can't wait to learn about the dawn of heroes!

The exhibit Midoriya set his sights on was all about those stalwart individuals who had taken a stand before there were any formal systems or regulations for heroes. The world might have turned out quite differently if not for them, which made this event worth turning down a day at a theme park. Still, he couldn't help but feel a little guilty.

Sorry, Ida!

But for Midoriya, nothing trumped heroes—that is, people who took action to save others. It was that concept that had taken root in his heart at some point, to the extent that his drive to become a hero was as foregone a conclusion as breathing.

No one can ever top All Might, though!

As a child, Midoriya had watched All Might's debut video clip over and over; sometimes with joy in his heart, at other times with tear-filled eyes as he shook the computer screen. He wished he could go back and tell his younger self that he would someday not only meet his idol but be granted his heart's desire—a Quirk of his own. His good fortune seemed too good to be true, so the boy was more than willing to run

himself ragged now, if that's what it took. He still couldn't control his inherited Quirk at 100 percent power, but he knew he'd get there eventually.

"Just gotta keep at it!"

"The hell?" came a thorny response to Midoriya's self-directed pep talk.

"Whoa! Kacchan!"

"Dammit, Deku, who said you could run into me!" spat Katsuki Bakugo as he came around the corner. The teasing during their early years as playmates had grown as the boys had, eventually turning into outright contempt on Bakugo's part. They kept out of each other's way as much as possible nowadays, but the bully's bad attitude towards Midoriya had deep roots.

"Sorry, I, um…"

His classmate ignored him and kept walking. With a small sigh, Midoriya left the tranquil residential area and realized he had a pit stop to make.

Right. Better hit up a convenience store for a drink before getting on the train. One of the ones with the All Might Mini-Mini collectible figures attached to the cap. Only need one more for the complete set…but the Silver Age version just won't turn up…

"Come to think of it, I'll pick up *Heroes Monthly* too. Can't miss that special feature on All Might. There's s'posed to be an interview and never-before-seen pics of him in action, so that should be cool! Also, the revised edition of *Complete Hero Works* that they said was coming out at the end of the month… Did I bring enough cash for all that? Hmm… Guess I could skip lunch today… But I do need to get my protein in."

"Quit mumbling behind my back—it's freaking weird!"

Midoriya's inadvertent switch to external monologue pushed Bakugo's buttons like nothing else.

"And stop following me, you damn stalker!" snapped the latter, grabbing the former by his collar.

"N-not following you! Just heading to the store for…"

"Well, I was headed there first, so you better wait till I'm done!" said Bakugo, releasing Midoriya with a shove and marching off again.

That's just unreasonable!

Not that pointing this out had ever fazed Bakugo.

Midoriya let loose another sigh and decided to do his shopping at the store near the station instead. He

kept walking, but his footsteps didn't go unnoticed.

"What'd I just say...?!" raged Bakugo as he spun around once more.

"I'm going to the station, and this is the quickest route."

"Like I care! Take the long way around, cuz I ain't having you in front of me or behind me!"

Okay then... How about shoulder to shoulder?

Unimaginable. The very thought sent a chill down Midoriya's spine.

Just gotta put up with him as far as the store...

But that was still a ways off, and Bakugo was promising to make the trip an awkward one. Midoriya stared as his classmate hurried ahead.

Watching him from behind, just like the old days, I guess.

Always filled with supreme confidence, Bakugo had led the other children around like a pint-sized general. Midoriya had enjoyed following him back when there was something reassuring about his cool childhood friend's leadership.

When'd it all turn south...?

He stopped brooding with a shake of his head and

turned to the other thing on his mind.

The letter. Right. Better write that once I get home. Gotta thank Mom for everything she does... I know I'm grateful, but how to put that in a letter? It's like...writing about it's just going to worry her more, probably.

Being born Quirkless had long been a source of angst for Midoriya. Fretting over it wouldn't achieve anything, but he could never help himself.

Maybe Mom was actually more anxious about it than I was...

He recalled his mother's tear-filled apology at the time.

Not like it was her fault, though.

With new vision for how he might approach the letter, Midoriya decided to consult Bakugo.

"Hey, Kacchan. You write that letter for Parents' Day yet?"

"Why? You picturing me writing some schmaltzy crap?"

Schmaltzy? I wonder what he thinks I think he'd write.

"Wipe that grin off your stupid mug!" said Bakugo, his own face contorting to match his tone.

"D-didn't mean it like that... What's your approach though? It's due tomorrow..."

"Just half-ass it! 'Thanks for giving birth to me, blah blah blah.'"

"That sounds, uh, insincere..."

"Huhh?! Then don't freaking ask me, dammit!" burst Bakugo at Midoriya's chiding. A small explosion in his palm showed he meant it.

"Geez, never mind, sorry!"

UA

While a flustered Midoriya was heading for the station, an eager Tenya Ida was putting on a headband with bunny ears.

"Perfect weather for a day at the theme park! Don't you agree, Kaminari? Mineta? Tokoyami?" exclaimed Ida, gazing at the clear skies. Beside him, his three classmates wore bear ears, elephant ears, and monkey ears, respectively.

Courtesy of Native's gift, the four boys found themselves at Zoo Dreamland—a theme park with a wildlife motif. With mock forest and savannah zones, among others, the park was popular with patrons of all ages. Sundays especially brought out the families, and like Ida and his classmates, most visitors were wearing animal ears.

When Midoriya and Todoroki had turned him down, Ida had been at a loss until he'd passed Mineta and Kaminari on his way home and extended the invite. They were on board, leaving one more ticket until Tokoyami had come along and, surprisingly, expressed interest.

"President, are these accessories really necessary?" asked Tokoyami, whose first-ever visit to a theme park had him questioning the animal ears.

"Not necessary, per se, but embracing the park's theme is sure to make the experience all the more delightful! We became 'wild' inhabitants of Zoo Dreamland the moment we stepped through the gates! Besides, look! The families who've come today are also enjoying the headbands!"

There was no stopping Ida's assuredness, though the sight of monkey ears on the bird-headed Tokoyami was more than a bit unsettling—a fact the latter

seemed to be aware of as he fiddled with the accessory. Still, the ever-serious Ida took a regimented approach to fun, even in a place like this.

"If that's how it is…" said Tokoyami with a nod, apparently convinced by Ida's passion. Meanwhile, Kaminari grew excited as he watched a pair of girls wearing rabbit ears pass by.

"It's just the gimmick here. And c'mon— girls with animal ears are cute as heck! Those bunnies, especially!"

"You want cute? Try a stuffed animal. Ears don't matter when the girls're missing what really counts!"

"Oh yeah? What really counts, then?" asked Kaminari, confused by Mineta's outburst.

"No bunny girl is complete without the whole costume! Boobs practically spilling out, a leotard cut at a sweet angle down there, and fishnet stockings for days! You'd think this 'Dreamland' would do a better job making dudes' dreams come true!" insisted Mineta with clenched fists, but Ida wasn't having it.

"Think about what you're implying, Mineta. What would rabbit women be doing in forest or savannah biomes?"

"It could happen! Maybe some of the working bunnies down in Shinjuku's Kabukicho neighborhood got snatched up by traffickers and released onto the savannah. Anything's possible… Just gotta apply that Plus Ultra attitude to your imagination!"

If all heroes needed was a dirty mind, Mineta would've already gone pro. However, Ida's straight man persona was more than a match for his classmate.

"And why would they release said women onto the tropical grasslands of either Africa or South America? What would your traffickers possibly have to gain by doing that?"

"Just saying it's possible! Maybe they've got a Kabukicho in Africa, too!"

"What? You mean to say there's a region in Africa named for the art of Japanese dance drama?"

"No! I'm talking red-light districts, man!"

"Whoa, cool it, you two. There're families around," said Kaminari.

Sure enough, the boys' argument had attracted unwanted attention—parents with children were staring from a cautious distance.

"P-pardon us! We're so very sorry for disturbing

you on your peaceful day off!"

At Ida's frantic apology and bow, the onlookers gave a few strained smiles before moving on with their day. The class president raised his head with renewed resolve.

"That was inexcusable, friends! Now that we're in Zoo Dreamland, we must put aside thoughts of the outside world and enjoy the park as we're meant to! Where to start, though? By the day's end, I hope to have conquered every last ride and attraction!"

Ida unfolded a map of the park to begin planning the itinerary, but behind him, Mineta and Kaminari locked eyes, paused, and gave each other subtle nods.

"Why don't we start with the Jungle Zone and…"

"Yo, President! Me and Mineta, there's a thing we wanna see."

The first shot came from Kaminari, and Mineta provided him with cover fire.

"Yeah, there's, uh, a hero event in the Savannah Zone! It's gonna start any minute now!"

"A hero event, you say? Then we ought to begin there…" said Ida, instantly convinced. He returned to

the map to chart a new route, but the other two shook their heads.

"D-don't sweat it! We can just split up!"

"Kaminari and me, President Ida and Tokoyami!"

But Ida noted their unnaturally eager smiles and grew suspicious.

"After we decided to come here together...?"

"But you won't get to 'conquer' every ride or whatever if you're babysitting us! And they'll probably sell out of that exclusive apple pie Tokoyami wanted!"

"That would be disappointing," murmured Tokoyami. In fact, Zoo Dreamland's limited-time apple pie was the reason he'd agreed to come in the first place.

"Hmm, you may have a point."

"They'd better not sell out."

Having planted the seed of doubt in Tokoyami, Mineta and Kaminari gave one final push.

"Great, so we'll meet back up at lunch!"

"Later!"

With that, the pair ran off at top speed.

"They sure want to attend that hero event badly."

"Which hero is coming, anyhow?"

"I don't know. I wasn't even aware of the event."

They watched their classmates dash away, and Ida suddenly remembered what really mattered.

"Oh no, your apple pie! The exclusive treat is available...here, at Forest Sweets."

"Let's go."

After confirming the location on the map, they set off. Ida had the confidence of someone who'd walked the route before, and he led them straight to the apple-themed shop. Before long, both boys were at a table with pies and drinks in hand.

"Mm. Good."

"Indeed. The cinnamon brings out the apples' sweetness while preserving the refreshing acidity, and the pie crust meshes perfectly with the baked apples' softened texture... Delicious."

While chewing, Tokoyami nodded at Ida's assessment. He then took another bite, adroitly navigating his beak into the pie. Seeing Tokoyami enjoy the treat only enhanced the experience for Ida.

"We ought to tell Kaminari and Mineta about this later. It'd be a shame if they missed out on something so good. But, Tokoyami—I have to say—I had no idea you loved apples so much."

"They claim the nutrition found in a single apple, if eaten daily, is enough to eliminate visits to the doctor, you know. Plus, that perfect combination of sweet and tart. And they can be preserved for long periods of time… There's no fruit more perfect than the apple."

Ida took it all in and gave a curt nod as he continued to eat.

"But you prefer oranges, don't you, President?" said Tokoyami, glancing at Ida's orange juice.

"Not exactly. Rather, their juice is like gasoline for me, so I never pass up a chance to drink some."

Ida's Quirk was "Engine"—the engine-like structures bulging from his calves allowed him to move at high speeds. His optimal fuel? One hundred percent pure orange juice. It wasn't that he was never in the mood for other drinks, but when the desire hit to buy canned coffee from a vending machine, say, Ida would nevertheless find himself pushing the button for orange juice. He never knew when he might need to spring into action, so it was better to be safe than sorry.

"Where to next? Any rides you're interested in, Tokoyami?"

Tokoyami was on the verge of finishing his pie, so Ida spread the park map out on the table.

"Not especially. Up to you, President."

"Very well... I know just the thing, then."

The boys started toward the next destination and soon found themselves in a wooded area. An elaborate series of sculptures occupied the gaps between the trees, including a tire, a giant melon bread, a pyramid, and a red sphere.

"What a bizarre space."

"I understand the park director is a patron of the arts, so for years now, there have been temporary installations around here. When I came as a child, I once spotted a troupe of performing gymnasts in this very spot, their bodies painted white from head to toe."

Tokoyami much preferred the current sculptures to what Ida described.

The pair soon reached their goal—a massive saucer-shaped base, filled with teacups just the right size for a few riders each.

"What am I looking at?"

"Oasis Teatime, they call it. The first essential stop

during any visit to the park! And look, no line! This is our chance, Tokoyami."

Ida raced for a cup, and his friend followed, noting that the only other riders were parents with small children.

"What does this handle do, President?" asked Tokoyami, indicating a circular grip in the center of their chosen cup.

"The faster we spin this, the faster the entire teacup rotates."

"Is that something we want?"

"Yes... Oh, it's starting!"

A buzzer sounded, and a languid carnival tune soon followed. Ida saw the surrounding children's faces break out in smiles, but his own face suddenly whipped sideways.

"T-Tokoyami...?!"

Tokoyami was spinning the central handle with every ounce of his strength, and Ida imagined he might be sent flying by the centripetal force.

"W-what are you doing...?" cried Ida, clinging on for dear life as his companion devoted himself to the assigned task.

"The goal of this ride is to spin the teacup, right…? I would say we're winning!"

I-it doesn't work that way!

That was what Ida meant to shout, anyway, but the words never made it out. The violent spinning sent the slurry of orange juice and pie in his stomach sloshing about.

A few minutes later, both boys slumped onto a bench, completely limp. Ida explained that spinning the teacups wasn't a competition, to which Tokoyami shook his head and replied, "You should've spoken up sooner…"

"So this really is your first visit to a theme park?"

"Why would I lie…? And what's next, President?"

"Recovered already, have you?"

"I'm not 100 percent, but you did say you wanted to conquer every attraction."

"In that case…how about something a bit calmer?"

They staggered and stumbled over to a gaudy merry-go-round. Since this was Zoo Dreamland, the usual horses were joined by rhinoceroses, lions, elephants, and the like. Ida chose a horse, Tokoyami, a rhino. The ride's slow spin came with leisurely music, and the

boys noticed parents with video cameras surrounding the merry-go-round, hoping to capture memories of their delighted children.

"How exactly is this fun, President?"

"Why, you can't tell, Tokoyami? These are animals one normally wouldn't get to ride, but here, it's perfectly safe. Look—the children seem to appreciate it."

And so the merry-go-round spun on, lit up by gentle sunbeams and excited cries.

"Why do so many of these rides involve spinning?" came the second blunt question from Tokoyami.

"That's not all there is. Some also move up and down while rotating."

"So, more spinning."

ⓤⓐ

As Tokoyami was slightly regretting his decision to come, a pair of hunters sat on a bench elsewhere.

"Hey. Mineta. How about those two in the bunny ears, huh?"

"Don't make the cut. Their faces are eights, but

style? Only sixes. The angels we're hunting need cute faces, great style, and killer personalities, and they gotta be naive enough to come hopping when we call!"

The girls in question were enjoying some ice cream just out of earshot as Kaminari and Mineta sized them up. The boys likely would've gotten an earful of "As if you're such prizes" had they been overheard.

This was why the two Casanovas had really come to the theme park—to pick up girls. The instant Ida had extended the invitation, the park was doomed to become their hunting grounds. They had plotted in advance to ditch Ida, since they knew the all-too-serious class president would lay down the law if he were to discover their true intentions.

While judging passing women, Kaminari voiced a concern.

"Hang on. What do we say to the other two if this actually works?"

"'Oh no, we seem to have come down with sudden stomachaches...' Then we ditch Zoo Dreamland and head off to Dirty Dreamland!"

The concept of friendship with Ida and Tokoyami had long since taken a back seat in these hunters' minds.

A pretty, fashionable woman appeared, glancing around anxiously.

"Look, our angel! The ideal prey!"

They couldn't have known anything about her personality or naivete, but Mineta's and Kaminari's eyes lit up at the sight of a potential prize. She was almost too good, though, and the hunters grew timid.

"W-what do we even say...?" asked Mineta. His partner in crime paused before answering.

"W-well, how about... 'Can we have a moment of your time?'"

"Too stiff, man! What, are you asking her to take a survey?"

"You do it, then!"

"Idiot! Compared to me, you're a teeny-tiny bit cooler, like by a nanometer! You gotta be the one!"

"If you put it that way... Say no more."

"Remember—*nano*'s even smaller than *milli*, okay?"

"What is this, math class? Just sit back and watch me work!"

"No, dummy! A girl's gonna be on guard against a cool dude like you! You need a nonthreatening cutie-pie like me to come along! But still, you gotta talk to her."

"I'm on it!"

With the nanometer compliment boosting his confidence, Kaminari stepped towards the woman, and Mineta followed.

"Hi there. Nice weather we're having, yeah?"

"Eh? Um, sure…" she replied, puzzled.

"You, uh, wanna hang out with us? We two dudes could use some company."

"Ah… No, I'm good…"

"Hey there! The name's Mineta! Don't worry—we seriously just wanna hang out, that's all!"

"No thanks, really…"

But the boys' flames were fanned by the woman's frustration, which somehow only made her more charming to them.

"Y-you hungry, maybe? We could go get that limited-time apple pie?"

"Yeah, it'll be our treat! But they'll sell out if we don't get there fast! C'mon… Ooh, such soft hands."

Just as the moonstruck Mineta gripped her hand to lead her away, a firm voice said, "Hey, mitts off my girl!"

"There you are, Ken!"

The apparent boyfriend came over carrying a paper

bag, and one intimidating glare from him was enough to petrify Mineta and Kaminari.

"You got some stones, trying to pick up another guy's girl..."

Threatened by this man-eating bear, the hunters turned into a pair of trembling baby bunnies.

"Whaaat? 'Pick up'? No way! We were just asking directions!"

"We're just simple folk from the countryside, y'see—wouldn't know a roller coaster if it bit us!"

"I ain't buying it..."

The woman turned to her enraged boyfriend with tears in her eyes.

"It's all your fault for walking off, Ken! Leaving me alone, and on my birthday date, no less..."

"Sorry, babe... I was just getting you this..."

Her eyes lit up as she removed the contents of the paper bag.

"Aww! The kangaroo plushie I wanted so bad..."

"Check inside the pouch..."

"Eh. A ring... Are you...?"

"Be mine, forever...?"

"Oh, Ken!"

Watching the live proposal, the two scared rabbits muttered "C-congratulations" and scampered off.

"We just saw an actual, off-line love story," said a weary Kaminari. Going from girl hunting to bearing witness to a marriage proposal had given them whiplash as good as any roller coaster might have.

"Makes me mad just thinking about it! Why do couples gotta come out in public at all? Let 'em have their lovey-dovey lives at home, outta my sight!"

"For real, though—aren't most of the cute, stylish girls gonna have boyfriends already?"

"That's...probably true."

"So maybe we'll have better luck going after plainer ones with fashion sense that's only so-so?"

Mineta crinkled his face at Kaminari's suggestion, giving it careful consideration.

"Skip the smoking hotties and go for more average girls, huh? Truth is, I do get nervous around real beauties, and it sucks. But I know I can bring my A game if we're talking plain Janes... Yeah, good point. Let's lower our standards."

Thus did Mineta make his declaration, with all the gravitas of a presidential speech.

However…

"Excuse you."

"This is a prank show, right?"

"Buzz off!"

A series of rejections from women Mineta and Kaminari deemed "average," likely put off by Mineta's overwhelming creep aura.

"But why? Even the plain ones!"

"Mineta, maybe we didn't lower our standards enough…"

"Yeah. Anything goes now, long as they've got a rack! Doesn't need to be Yaoyorozu class! Even flat as Jiro is fine at this point!"

Once hunters, then rabbits, and now a pair of starved hounds, they started catcalling every passing woman of reasonable age.

Still, though…

"No thanks."

"Yeah, no."

"Um, bye."

"I'm here with my boyfriend."

"I'm gonna call the police, 'kay?"

Stripped of even the energy to remain standing after this series of defeats, the hounds slumped onto a bench and decried the harsh truths of the natural world.

"Even the buckshot approach failed...and I'm all outta ammo..."

"Why, God, why?!"

As Kaminari grumbled and Mineta questioned the Almighty, the former's phone buzzed with a text from Ida. They'd whiled away the hours, and it was already past noon. The weary hounds reluctantly agreed to meet back up with the other two and left the bench.

"Guess it'll just be us four guys at the theme park... This day's seriously lacking boobs. Well, no other choice... Kaminari—stick two of my Pop Off balls on your chest."

Mineta's Quirk, "Pop Off," gave him a clump of bumpy protuberances covering his head. The soft, squishy balls could be plucked away and stuck onto nearly anything.

"Gah! What I wouldn't give for a good reverse pickup! Y'know? Girls hitting on guys!"

"Impossible. That's just an urban legend, man."

But contrary to Mineta's belief, the Lord had not abandoned these two.

"Umm, hello..."

A reverse pickup, really...?!

Upon hearing the cute, young-sounding voice behind them, the boys started breathing heavily and spun around.

"Yo! We're just a couple of guys looking to pass the time and... Huh? Nobody there?"

Kaminari was speaking to empty air.

"Kaminari... Down here," said Mineta, clearly flustered.

"Down...? Eh?"

At Kaminari's feet stood a little girl wearing a headband with giraffe horns and ears.

UA

"So, you discovered a lost child named Yuka."

"I'm not lost! Big girls in kindergarten don't get lost!"

Kaminari and Mineta had brought Yuka to the rendezvous with the other two, and through pursed lips, she clearly took issue with Ida's assessment of her situation. As she told it, she'd come to the park with her mother, but when her mother went to buy lunch, Yuka had spotted her favorite costumed character, followed it, and then couldn't find her way back.

"See? We can't argue there," said Kaminari with a weak smile. "She doesn't want us bringing her to the lost-child center."

"That's cuz I'm not a lost child, mister. I just dunno where I'm s'posed to meet my mommy."

"Right. You are literally a lost child."

Yuka shrank at Tokoyami's reasonable point and scurried behind Kaminari, surprising everyone.

"You've kinda been giving our Tokoyami the cold shoulder," pointed out Mineta. In hushed tones, the frightened girl explained.

"B-birds are scary... One time one ate my bread and bit me."

Kaminari and Mineta burst out laughing.

"Is that all? Tokoyami's no bird. He just looks that way cuz of his Quirk."

"His Quirk...?" asked the girl, still scared, but now glancing at Tokoyami curiously.

"Sorry for laughing—I get that it must've been scary. I got pecked by a crow once, too."

"Yuka, Tokoyami here is an absolute gentleman. You have nothing to fear."

"But…"

Tokoyami sighed.

"Psychological scars don't heal that easily. Anyhow, her mother is probably worried about her."

"Indeed. We ought to bring her to her designated meeting spot at once, as that might resolve everything," said Ida, nodding at Tokoyami. "Now, where were you supposed to meet in case you got lost, Yuka?"

"In front of the apple!" shouted the girl, implying that this was all she could remember.

"The apple? Near where they were selling apple pies, maybe? Was there an actual apple there?"

"Yes, there were most assuredly apple decorations near Forest Sweets. We should head back there."

So the four boys and the girl started towards the sweets shop. Yuka was glued to Kaminari—hand in hand—as he was the one farthest from Tokoyami. Glancing around, an awkward expression arose on Kaminari's face.

"Sure hope nobody thinks we're kidnappers or something…"

"Why would they, Kaminari?"

"Four guys with one little girl? We make for a weird group."

"If they catch you, I'll just tell the truth, so don't worry, okay?"

"Cool. Thanks, Yuka."

"Sheesh. Finally a reverse pickup, but it had to be a pip-squeak?"

"Reverse pickup? What are you talking about?"

Mineta and Kaminari panicked at Ida's question.

"Nothing! Forget it!"

"'Reverse pickup'? Who said that? Nobody!"

But Yuka spoke up.

"Umm, yeah, they said it before too. 'I want a good reverse pickup.' 'Just an ur-bann legend.' So what's a reverse pickup, anyway?"

"Seriously not important, right, Kaminari?"

"Y-yeah, I mean, y'know, kids these days say some shocking things, ha ha ha!"

Despite their attempt to dodge, Ida wasn't having it.

"Kaminari. Mineta. As teenagers, it's your duty to answer the child's innocent question. I'm ashamed to

admit I don't understand the phrase either, so why don't you educate both Yuka and myself?"

Locking eyes with Ida, Kaminari and Mineta were at a loss for words. They had the answer, of course, but telling the truth wasn't a viable option here. The stares from the deadly serious class president and purehearted girl forced Kaminari to say something.

"A reverse pickup is when, like, uh... You pick up... in...reverse, and..."

He short-circuited, and it had nothing to do with his Quirk, "Electrification." Realizing he had to act, Mineta desperately latched on to a lie and rolled with it.

"Reverse pickup... Right! Like when you call and order takeout but then go and pick it up!"

Ida still wasn't biting.

"I see... Except that's a perfectly ordinary thing to do, no? I fail to see where the 'reverse' part comes into the equation. And you 'want a good reverse pickup'? Were you thinking of ordering food while at the theme park?"

"Sometimes you're just in the mood for it, yeah...?"

"No, I can't say I've ever had the urge to call and place an order for takeout while out and about. What on earth would put you in that mood, Mineta?"

"When I'm feeling lonely?"

"Ah, so lonely that you're desperate to place the call, speak to the restaurant employee, and then see them in person for the all-important pickup? Nonsense, Mineta! Why not just go out to eat or have it delivered and make small talk with the courier?"

"You just wouldn't get it…"

"And how exactly is this reverse pickup an urban legend…?"

"Uh… Cuz, like…"

Seeing Mineta stumbling, Tokoyami muttered, "Backed into a corner, then," prompting Yuka to gasp and hide behind Kaminari. Another sigh from Tokoyami. It was a shame that his appearance scared her like this, but there was nothing he could do about how he was born.

"Explain, Mineta."

Forced by Ida to concoct a story about getting lonely and ordering food, Mineta wanted to fire back with "An urban legend's just that! Up to you to believe it or not!" but he didn't have the guts.

"I see. You're not sure either, Mineta. We'll have to

do some research later."

Mineta and Kaminari breathed subtle sighs of relief, glad that their classmate had decided to drop the issue, but Yuka stared at Mineta in awe.

"Mister Bumpy Head knows a lot about a lot of stuff, huh."

"Hey, is that the best nickname I can get?"

"Ha ha. 'Bumpy Head.' What does that make me, Yuka?"

"You're Mister Blond."

Ida observed the exchange and smiled.

"You two are wonderful with children, it seems. Perhaps because you're so approachable? That's an essential quality for any good hero."

"Y'think?"

"That's cuz kids can tell what a great big heart I've got! I mean, not saying yours is small or anything, Tokoyami! No offense."

"Absolutely none taken."

Kaminari blushed, Mineta soaked up the praise, and Tokoyami couldn't care less. Seeing her saviors looking so upbeat, Yuka beamed and spoke.

"You guys were talking with all those ladies before,

right? You told them, 'We got nothing to do, so let's hang out'—which's why I thought you could tell me where to go!"

Gaaah!

The rotten truth, laid bare by a child's innocence.

"I was under the impression that you two attended a hero event of some sort...?"

Under the bunny ears, Ida's expression turned grim.

"After splitting up with us, you went to pick up girls, right?" asked Tokoyami, long since fed up with the entire situation.

"No, we, uh..."

"Pick...up...?"

Ida gasped.

"Could the pickup of your 'reverse pickup' be the 'pick' and 'up' of 'picking up girls'? Why did you say it meant ordering food?!"

"Just stop saying 'pickup' already," said Kaminari, unable to help himself despite the predicament.

"It's because of you two that we're saying any of this! Outrageous, that you would misinform a child as you have! Listen, Yuka. 'Reverse pickup' has nothing to do with ordering takeout. It must be the opposite of 'pick-

ing up women,' which means that these two were hoping that women might pick them up."

Ida crouched as he passionately explained everything to Yuka, but Tokoyami had other thoughts.

"Maybe she doesn't need to know all this."

"No, even children must be taught these things. It won't do her any good to grow up misinformed," said Ida, shaking his head at an unnatural angle and causing the bunny ears to flop around. Yuka responded to his earnestness in kind.

"Okay, Mister Glasses. I'll remember! But what's 'picking up,' anyway?"

"It's a colloquialism that refers to the practice of men approaching women they've never met, on the street, and asking them to be friends. When women approach men, they apparently call it a 'reverse pickup.'"

"So I did a reverse pickup!"

"No, Yuka. We're talking about requests to, erm, enjoy each other's company. You, on the other hand, were lost and needed directions."

"Oh, too bad."

"Nothing bad about it, Yuka! Because to start with, Mineta and Kaminari were pestering women at a place of wholesome family fun. Scoundrels, aren't they? True romance comes from knowing one another, slowly taking the time to forge real bonds, and going on to start a family, even…"

Upon hearing Ida's sober ethical viewpoint, amateur admirer of the female form Mineta couldn't hold back.

"You can shove your true romance! I just wanna be the biggest scoundrel I can while I'm still young!"

"Mister Blond, what's a scown-drul?"

"Don't look at me, kid."

"Hey. We're at Forest Sweets," interrupted Tokoyami, prompting Ida and Mineta to call a temporary cease-fire on their moral debate. Just as Ida had remembered, there were plenty of apple-themed decorations promoting the exclusive pie.

"Is this where your mother told you to find her, Yuka?"

"No, not here. A way bigger apple, like…thiiis big," replied a troubled Yuka, stretching her arms as far as she could.

"You know any bigger apples around here, President?"

"I frequented Zoo Dreamland as a child, but no, I don't recall any giant apples... And nothing on the map hints at anything like that."

"I'm never gonna see my mommy again...?"

Seeing tears well up in the girl's eyes, the boys panicked. As hero hopefuls, the thought of making a child weep tears of anything but gratitude was outrageous.

"I-I know! Maybe we can spot this apple from somewhere up high?"

"Excellent idea! Where can we find such a vantage point...?"

"I got it—the Ferris wheel!" cried Mineta, pointing at the tallest structure in all of Zoo Dreamland.

"Another one that spins..." grumbled Tokoyami.

They were aboard the ride within minutes.

"Yuka, take a good look and try to find your meeting spot."

"Okay!"

Their pod rose higher and higher, and all five were glued to the windows, scanning the park.

"Some sort of eyesight Quirk would come in real handy right about now. Too bad my Electrification is basically useless."

"My Quirk isn't suited to searching, either," said Ida, nodding at Kaminari.

"What's your Quirk, Mister Glasses...?"

"It's Engine, and it allows me to run quickly."

"Ohh, cool. I don't have my Quirk yet," said the girl, looking dejected.

"This's my Quirk. Here, have one."

"Don't want it," she said with a shake of her head, turning down one of Mineta's head balls.

"Seriously? But they're super sticky! Check it out!"

Dissatisfied with the blunt rejection, Mineta stuck the ball to the wall. Tokoyami shot him a dark look.

"Stop that—you're rocking the boat."

"This is hardly the time for that, Mineta! We need to locate the giant apple!"

In the end, though, they came up with nothing. Even the park employees they asked didn't have a clue.

"Let's just try the lost-child center, yeah?" suggested Kaminari, but the girl shook her head dramatically.

"There was no uh-nouns-ment though, so that means Mommy didn't go there yet."

"Maybe she went home already?" offered Mineta, but his clumsy suggestion only made Yuka bawl.

"Dammit, Mineta!"

"Just kidding! Of course she didn't leave without you!"

"Show some tact."

"Why joke about that with a little kid?"

"Tch, I'm pretty little myself! Lay off me... Wait a sec!"

Mineta ran off and returned a moment later with a red balloon.

"Look! A big, red apple!" he shouted, but Yuka cut him off.

"Too small! A way, way bigger apple than that one!"

"'That one'?"

"Uh-huh," said Yuka, nodding.

"Silly Yuka. That's a balloon. Apples are fruits," laughed Kaminari.

"No, if it's round and red, then it's an apple!"

The four boys froze and looked at each other.

"So we may simply be looking for a round red object!"

"Big? Round? Red...? Have we seen anything like that?"

Kaminari's question triggered Tokoyami's memory of the red spherical sculpture in the forest zone.

"We have. This way."

"Eh?"

Yuka looked up at Tokoyami as he raced off.

"Slow down, Tokoyami! Come now, Yuka. Let's fol-
low him!"

They arrived at the red sphere and, sure enough, found
the anxious mother waiting.

"Mommy!"

"Oh, Yuka! Where were you? Mommy was worried
half to death…"

They embraced, and after a brief explanation from
the boys, the mother showered them with apologies
and appreciation.

"We only did what was right, ma'am. No need to
thank us."

"No getting lost again, okay, Yuka?"

"Feel free to try that reverse pickup once you're,
like, twenty."

"Uh…"

"Say thank you to the nice young men, Yuka."

"Thanks, misters!"

The boys waved goodbye and started to walk off, but Yuka chased after Tokoyami.

"M-Mister Bird!"

"What is it?"

"Um… Sorry for getting scared of you… You're way bigger than that other bitey bird, so I thought you were gonna eat me up with that big beak."

Tokoyami chuckled at the timid girl.

"You've no cause to worry about that, because my favorite food is apples."

At Tokoyami's smile, the girl's cheeks blushed, red and round.

After a late lunch, the four boys trekked back to Forest Sweets for dessert. The plan was for Kaminari and Mineta to get pies, since they hadn't earlier, but Tokoyami went for seconds (it was as if he had a second stomach for anything apple) and Ida followed suit.

"Still just as delicious."

At Tokoyami's side, Ida suddenly remembered something.

"Ah, have you all written your letters yet?"

"Oh yeah. That. I jotted down some stuff... But do we really gotta read them in front of our parents? What, they couldn't think of something more embarrassing for us?"

"Ugh, and tomorrow's the big day. What a drag."

Ida's eyes sprang wide at the groaning Mineta.

"It's hardly a drag, Mineta! Think of it as a golden opportunity to tell your family how much you appreciate them! Why, I've already penned over forty pages' worth of gratitude."

"The hell? I only wrote two."

"I've got one."

"You managed to say all you needed with that little?" chided Ida.

"You basically represent the whole class, President, so we'd all love to hear yours. In fact, you should be the only one to read out loud, I say."

Kaminari's suggestion was one part genuine, one

part desperate, but Ida shook his head solemnly.

"That would never do... I suppose, though, that my forty pages would eat into everyone else's time... Hmm. I'll need to make my thoughts more concise!"

While Ida pondered, Tokoyami stared affectionately at his final bite of pie before it disappeared into his beak. Just then, security personnel raced past the boys.

"Wonder what's going on?"

They looked towards the scene and heard a series of crashes and screams. Sensing that something out of the ordinary was afoot, the U.A. students got up and started running.

The source of the commotion was the haunted house, now surrounded by rubberneckers.

"Get back, get back, people!"

"I think my baby's still in there... Yuka didn't make it out!"

"Hey, that's Yuka's mother!" said Ida, recognizing the woman pleading with security. The high schoolers weaved through the crowd and made it over to her.

"Oh, it's you boys..."

"What on earth is happening? Is Yuka okay...?"

The woman looked ready to burst into tears.

"The two of us were walking through the haunted house, but then Yuka disappeared…and the monster puppets, they…"

She was cut off by another crash from inside the attraction.

"Oh no, Yuka!"

No answer. Again, she begged the security guard to let her in.

"Just wait here, ma'am. We're trying to… Huhh?"

More noise from the haunted house, and the security guard's face twisted in terror. One of the puppets seemed to peer out from the entrance, floating and bobbing like a real-life ghost.

"Gaaah!"

"What the hell's going on…?"

Security was doing all it could to keep the crowd back.

"D-do not approach the attraction, people! And, ma'am—we've called in a hero to deal with the situation, so please just be patient."

"But my daughter…"

Torn somewhere between fight and flight, Yuka's

mother stared at the haunted house.

Zoo Dreamland was quite a distance from town, and with no nearby hero agencies, help wouldn't arrive for some time. Ida knew what he had to do.

"I will find your daughter, ma'am. Don't you worry."

"Eh?"

He smiled wide to reassure the frazzled mother, spun on his heel, and dove into the crowd. His three classmates followed.

"Not so fast, President. How're you planning on finding her?"

"By venturing inside, naturally," said Ida as they arrived at the rear of the haunted house.

"My brother once discovered a hidden passage. It was right around… Yes, here we are."

He crouched near a small window at the base of the black wall.

"By my brother's honor, I swear that I never once exploited this secret! I only came upon it by accident once, when I tripped and fell inside. If ever there were a time that such a thing could prove useful, though… There, it's open. I'll need to ask you three to stay here and keep wa—"

"Keep watch? What's the point? I'm coming in too."

"Seriously, Kaminari?"

"If that little girl's really still in there, then it's a race against time. And depending on what exactly is happening, the president might need all the help he can get."

"Kaminari, Tokoyami… You're absolutely right. Time spent wavering is time we cannot get back. Let's go."

With Ida taking point, the three boys crept through the opening.

"Dammit! Fine, I'll come along for the ride! We're still s'posed to be in training, though! We ain't real heroes just yet!" said a reluctant Mineta.

"Whoa. Sure is dark."

Once their eyes adjusted to the darkness, the destruction became apparent. Broken equipment and decorations lay strewn about as if a tornado had been taking a tour. In the dimly lit space, they heard something shuffling about. Several somethings.

"Y'think the guys who wear the monster costumes got fed up working in this dump and this is their idea of a labor strike…?" whimpered Mineta, trying to act

tough but unable to hide his terror. Ida grimaced at this, on high alert.

"No. This particular haunted house is meant for children, so the ghosts and monsters are all animatronic... Still, we did see that one, at the entrance."

"Yeah, how was that thing moving around on its own...?"

"That mystery comes later. First, we find the girl."

"I'm with you there, but... Gwaah?!"

Mineta didn't get to answer Tokoyami, because at that moment, an animatronic *kappa* attacked from above. The charming rendition of the mythical creature was meant to delight children, but in the poor lighting, there was something grotesque and otherworldly about it.

"Mineta!"

Kaminari screamed, and Tokoyami followed suit.

"Dark Shadow!"

With that, a shadow shaped like a mynah bird sprang from Tokoyami's body. It was his Quirk.

"Shaaaah!"

The familiar's shrill roar pierced the dim space, like that of a ferocious beast set loose from its cage. It tore into the kappa with aplomb, destroying the puppet in an instant.

"Eek!"

Mineta fell back, paralyzed, as Dark Shadow kept mauling the broken kappa.

"More… Need more prey!"

It swelled up, feeding itself on the surrounding darkness and sweeping from left to right, seeking out targets to attack. As a rule of thumb, Dark Shadow would become stronger in darker places, eventually forgetting Tokoyami altogether and transforming into an uncontrollable monster.

"Stop that, Dark Shadow!"

It ignored the command. The jet-black demon prowled the immediate area and continued the massacre until each and every puppet was in pieces.

"That's one scary pet you've got, Tokoyami!"

Mineta's cry caught Dark Shadow's attention. It stopped and swiveled slowly.

"Did you say 'pet'…?"

Hearing the note of rage in the question, Mineta shook his head violently.

"J-just kidding! You're actually the master, aren'tcha?"

"We are equals!" came the response from both Dark Shadow and Tokoyami in unison. The furious shade rushed at Mineta like a gale, dodging past Tokoyami. Ida shouted.

"Some light, Kaminari!"

"R-right!"

An instant before Dark Shadow reached Mineta, Kaminari's entire body lit up in a burst of electrified light.

"Kyaah!"

Bathed in Kaminari's glow, Dark Shadow shrunk back like a docile puppy.

"I was almost a goner."

"Well done, Kaminari! Keep that up, for now, as your light will make our search for Yuka all the easier."

"Gotcha!"

"Too bright..." yelped Dark Shadow at Tokoyami.

"Endure it, you."

"Where are you, Yuka? If you're there, give us a sign!"

But there was no response to Ida's plea. With all the animatronic puppets reduced to motionless scraps, the haunted house fell completely silent.

"Guess she just ain't in here? Maybe she ran out in the confusion and got lost again."

"She's here," objected the pacified Dark Shadow.

"You sure, Dark Shadow?"

"She's scared. Hiding in the dark."

"Guess a shadowy bird monster has its uses, huh."

"Can you sense where she is?"

"This way," said the familiar, floating towards a prop well in the corner. In front of the well was a headband with giraffe ears.

"Wasn't Yuka wearing that earlier?"

"She's in the well."

The four boys peered inside but found no one.

"You messing with us?"

"No!"

Tokoyami paused to think.

"Maybe her Quirk manifested?"

"Yuka's, you mean?"

"Yeah. Maybe she can meld with the dark and control objects in that same darkness. That would explain her disappearance, the destruction in here, everything."

"That'd make sense, if it happened to her all at once."

"Hey, Yuka! You'll be just fine! Come on out now!" shouted Ida into the well, but only the darkness stared back.

"Why won't she emerge?"

"She's panicking, probably. Everyone gets a little freaked out when their Quirk manifests, right? When it first happened to me, I shocked myself silly and couldn't think straight for a whole day. Yayyy."

Right on cue, Kaminari was reaching his limit.

"Same here. I panicked so much I plucked off balls till I bled."

"Maybe she can't figure out how to reverse the effects?"

"Allow me to try," said Tokoyami, turning towards the well's inky blackness.

"Calm yourself. Pacify your soul and become aware of your own consciousness. Then emerge from the darkness."

Kaminari took issue with Tokoyami's approach.

"Yayyy, Tokoyami. You're talking to a little kid, remember?

"Explain it in a more digestible way, Tokoyami! You're entirely too stiff! Too formal!"

"You know it's bad when President here is telling you to loosen up."

"What is that supposed to mean, Mineta?"

"Kettle, meet pot!"

Tokoyami paused again before reaching his hand into the well.

"Yuka. Take my hand."

A faded ghostly hand appeared out of the darkness and groped around before finding Tokoyami's. He gripped hard and pulled, and the rest of the girl popped out.

"Mister Bird…"

"You'll be okay now."

The boys rejoiced, and Ida said, "Your mother is worried sick about you! We must show her that you're all right."

But Yuka gave a small shake of her head.

"And why not?"

"Mommy got so scared… I got scared too… I hate the dark when I'm all alone…"

Watching the tears well up in Yuka's eyes, Tokoyami spoke.

"The darkness of this place revealed your true

nature. That is neither something to fear, nor to feel ashamed about."

"Too wordy, man!" said Kaminari

"What I mean to say is…"

Words failed Tokoyami, but Dark Shadow crept around from behind him, ready to assist.

"The dark is your friend!"

"Dark Shadow!"

"Who's…that…?"

"This guy happens to be my Quirk."

Yuka flinched at the sight of the shadow bird but then approached.

"You're not scared of it, Yuka?"

"Not if it's your friend. I'm not scared of you either anymore, Mister Bird."

"Glad to hear it."

"Friends, friends! I made friends!" said Yuka, smiling wide and prompting sighs of relief from the boys.

"Shall we be off, then?"

The five of them exited the haunted house just as the responding hero arrived, and after Ida's efficient play-by-play to the authorities, the scene calmed down. Apparently, the park's Quirk insurance would cover the cost of the damage to the attraction.

"I don't know what to say... This makes it twice now you boys have rescued my little Yuka."

The mother wanted a proper way to thank them, but Ida wasn't having it.

"No thanks necessary."

"I can think of one or two ways you could thank me, lady..."

"Mineta! Not in front of her kid, dammit!" cried Kaminari, disgusted by Mineta's desperate approach.

"As students at U.A. High School and aspiring heroes, we did what we had to do. Think nothing of it, ma'am!"

The grateful mother stared at the boys and placed her hands on her daughter's shoulders.

"These wonderful young men are your future heroes, Yuka."

"Thanks again, misters," said Yuka with a small bow, before running up to Tokoyami.

"Um... I, uh..."

"What's the matter?"

Blushing something fierce, Yuka stared up at Tokoyami awkwardly.

"You're a Prince Charming, Mister Bird I love you!"

Tokoyami's lower beak dropped, Yuka's mother said "Oh my," and Kaminari and Mineta scowled.

"Forget a reverse pickup—this guy just got a crush to confess!"

"What, we're s'posed to be jealous? She's a little kid, not a lady... But once she grows up... Damn! Why, God, why...?"

As Mineta cursed the heavens, Ida lectured the girl.

"Is that how you feel, Yuka...? It's a bit early for romance, though. Once you're all grown-up, you'll first need permission from your parents to date. Of course, you might want to ask Tokoyami's parents as well!"

"Okay, I'm gonna remember all that. Bye-bye, Mister Bird."

At Yuka's sparkling smile, Tokoyami's face gave every indication that he was blushing.

"The future is surely shrouded in darkness."

Part 5
Heartwarming Trio

Just as Mineta was being driven to tears of rage by Tokoyami's new admirer, Ochaco Uraraka was strolling towards the supermarket, reusable shopping bag in hand. She rattled off her shopping list while counting on her fingers—each of which had a distinctive padded tip.

"Discounted carrots, onions, peppers, eggs, milk... Ah, shallots too. Dad loves shallots and Worcestershire sauce with his curry... Crud! Also need to pick up the sauce!"

In order to attend U.A. High, Uraraka had moved away from home and was now living alone. Her folks ran a construction company, but contracts were scarce these days, so times were tough. In fact, Uraraka had set out to become a hero for financial reasons, hoping to give back to her parents for all they'd done for her.

Her father would be the one attending Parents' Day the next day, and Uraraka knew how much it would cost him just to make the trip out. She'd insisted that he didn't need to come, but he was determined to get a glimpse of his daughter's success all the same.

Uraraka pondered the Worcestershire sauce for a moment.

"I'll check the price, and if it's too much, Dad'll just have to do without!"

She loved her father, but her strict budgeting was nonnegotiable, especially when there was something even more important than curry add-ins on her shopping list. She plucked a supermarket flyer from her bag. Giant red discounts danced across the page, but it was a bit of plain black text in the corner that shone bright for Uraraka.

KUDO CUT MOCHI JUMBO PACK: ¥250!

The usual price of 600 yen was slashed by more than half, and the vacuum-sealed packaging made

this mochi last as long as it needed to. Most importantly, though, Uraraka was a die-hard mochi fan who couldn't pass up the opportunity. Unfortunately, the offer came with a fine print addendum.

*Limit: 1 Per Customer

"Stingy jerks!" said Uraraka out loud, her whole body puckering in annoyance. She knew the store just wanted as many people as possible taking advantage of the deal, but the typically upbeat girl's face darkened over her necessarily frugal lifestyle.

"At least make it two per person... No, three... Or four... Wait, five... Why not ten packs!"

Like a salesperson driving a hard bargain, Uraraka's fantasy pile of mochi packs grew higher and higher in her mind.

"What's the matter, Uraraka?"

"Ten packs of what, now?"

It was her classmates—Momo Yaoyorozu and Tsuyu Asui.

"Whoa! It's you two! Don't see this combo too often!" said Uraraka, tickled pink to run into the girls outside of school.

"I was out looking for reference books at the bookstore, and I happened upon Tsuyu on my way home."

Asui lifted some stationery out of her own shopping bag.

"And I needed more writing paper. Where are you headed, Ochaco?"

"Grocery shopping! My dad's coming tomorrow, so I gotta stock up."

"Right, you live alone, don't you, Uraraka? How impressive that you cook for yourself. It must be a chore sometimes?"

Uraraka blushed and chuckled at Yaoyorozu's praise.

"Wouldn't go that far, really. It's just that eating out or getting delivery adds up quick. Besides, I cut corners plenty. When I don't feel like really cooking, a single piece of mochi is enough..."

With that, Uraraka gasped, suddenly remembering her predicament.

"Oh no, the mochi!" she said, hanging her head in despair. Her classmates exchanged puzzled looks.

"What's this about mochi, then?"

"Well, y'see..."

Yaoyorozu's and Asui's blank stares turned to smiles as Uraraka explained.

"So that counting you were doing before—that was all about mochi packs?"

"That explains your furrowed brows as well."

"Cuz…for me, the difference between one and two, even, would be huge. We're talking about surviving a whole extra month for each pack."

Uraraka's cheeks reddened.

"Why don't we help you out, then? We can each buy a pack of mochi."

"Yes. I would be happy to assist if it's a matter of my classmate's survival."

"Goddesses in the flesh!" cried Uraraka in reverence, as if the heavens really had taken pity on her; she might've gone into full kowtow mode if her friends hadn't stopped her. They set off for the supermarket at a brisk pace, and Uraraka nearly began skipping.

"Three packs of mochi. Talk about luxury."

She seemed poised to lift off the ground in sheer delight—and not because she'd floated herself. But she could have, because Uraraka's Quirk was "Zero Gravity," which removed the effects of gravity from anything she touched, including her own body.

"You sure have a thing for mochi, Ochaco."

"Won't you tire of it, though? Day in, day out?"

"Don't be silly, Yaoyorozu! Every piece of mochi has unlimited potential! You can pair it with soy sauce, nori, nori and soy sauce and mayo, butter and soy sauce, sugar and soy sauce, kinako, natto, natto and kimchi, natto and kimchi and mayo, shredded radish, veggie soup, red bean soup, cheese…"

"I-I had no idea there were so many options… It seems I underestimated the power of mochi."

"And if you've got a sweet tooth, mochi also goes with chocolate, weirdly enough."

"With chocolate? Is that actually good?"

"I can hardly imagine it…"

"Something you can't imagine? That's a first, Yao-yorozu."

Yaoyorozu's Quirk, "Creation," allowed her body to create any nonliving thing so long as she understood the molecular structure.

"Perhaps I'd just rather not imagine it."

"Ah, I should treat you girls to some chocolate mochi as thanks for this favor!"

"Hrm, I might prefer a different variety…"

"Now I'm kind of curious to try it."

"You bet!"

The conversation went on, and they soon arrived at the supermarket. It was a large chain store, featuring not only the usual food staples but also a section with home goods and clothing.

"Let's do this, hmm?"

"So this is a 'supermarket'…"

Uraraka and Asui were already through the automatic doors with a shopping basket, but Yaoyorozu had stopped to glance around.

"Yaoyorozu?"

"Oh. Apologies. It isn't often I visit places like this…"

"That's our princess for ya!"

"Sh-shouldn't we use one of these carts…?" asked Yaoyorozu, indicating the shopping carts next to the baskets.

"Sure, why not."

Uraraka placed her basket into the slot in the cart and pushed it towards her mystified classmate, who looked as if she was witnessing something rare and fantastic.

"Wanna push?"

"Yes, may I? I've long been intrigued about these things, actually…"

An excited Yaoyorozu pushed the cart.

"How smooth! And convenient, too. It keeps the arms from tiring too quickly."

Asui's somewhat expressionless face twitched into something resembling a smile.

"You're like a little kid, Yaoyorozu."

"It's kinda cute!" agreed Uraraka with a nod as they reached the clothing area.

"Oh, I wasn't aware that supermarkets also sold clothing."

"No reason we can't take a look later, but first up is…"

"Securing the mochi. Yeah."

Uraraka knew the store best, so she led the way. Yaoyorozu—still with the cart—surveyed the vegetable displays in wonder.

"Uraraka, it seems there's an all-you-can-pack deal on carrots and potatoes! Pack into what, though? The shopping bag you brought?"

"Nah, these plastic ones. Don't want them accusing me of shoplifting!" quipped Uraraka, causing her friend to blush a bit.

"Right. Of course. I hear about that on TV now and then. 'Shoplifting.'"

"Yeah, it comes up on the evening news. Especially people with Quirks that can warp stuff away. They're hard to catch, which is a real problem if they're robbing smaller stores."

"Awful, huh. Small businesses already have enough on their plates without that," said Uraraka, who naturally had her own family in mind. Yaoyorozu gave a solemn nod.

"Larceny, yes. Violent crimes get more focus, but a crime is a crime, and all criminals should be dealt with. Too many people think only of themselves."

This gave Uraraka pause.

"Hang on. Given the whole one-per-person thing, should I really be asking you guys to help me get more mochi...?"

It was a serious concern, and the other two girls thought for a moment.

"It is something to consider... I can't say I've ever

faced a moral dilemma like this one…"

"My family pulls this trick all the time, but maybe it's different with friends? Does it count as a scam, you think?" asked Uraraka.

"Well, if you end up with more than you should, that means someone else is going without…maybe."

Asui's reasoned take threw Uraraka into head-clutching despair.

"Dangit… I'm s'posed to be a hero someday, but I put my own budgeting over other people and the mochi they deserve!"

"Poor Uraraka…"

"H-hey, isn't that the mochi?" asked Asui, pointing to a display a few paces away. Sure enough, massive bags of mochi were piled high.

"There's so much here, Ochaco. I don't think you should worry."

"Indeed. Removing three packs from all this is like a drop out of the bucket."

Encouraged by her friends, Uraraka said, "I-I guess," and tossed one pack into the cart. But the image of tipping scales stayed her hand as she reached for a second.

"Ugh. What if a bunch of big families are about to show up, planning a mochi party or something...? But then again, what about *my* mochi party, huh...? Just dunno."

"How about we wait a bit, and if this big pile's still here, we'll pick up another two packs? If the pile's shrunk, then we only take one more, and if there's barely any left, you limit yourself to that one," said Asui, offering her conflicted friend a suggestion.

"Excellent idea. I'm sure the store would prefer to sell out the lot."

"You two sure? I don't wanna make you wait around..."

"Fine by me."

"Me, as well. Besides which, I find this supermarket fascinating."

"Thanks, girls!"

Determined to kill some time, the trio wandered the store. They passed through the snacks aisle and debated their favorite childhood treats while moving towards the clothing area.

"You mentioned buying paper, Tsuyu? Was that for the Parents' Day letter?" asked Uraraka, while watching an excited Yaoyorozu fawn over the pajama section in wonderment.

"Yeah. I was running low on nice writing paper, and a letter's just not the same without it, you know? You finish writing yours yet, Ochaco?"

"Yep! Totally did! How about you, Yaoyorozu?"

"Eh? Yes, of course. Still, it's terribly embarrassing to imagine reading such a personal letter in front of everyone."

"I hear that. I'm worried my dad's gonna go overboard with his reaction," said Uraraka with a nervous smile.

"So it'll just be your dad coming, Ochaco?"

"Uh-huh. Mom wanted to come just as bad, but Dad was the winner after their discussion and a few rounds of rock-paper-scissors."

"It sounds as though your family gets along splendidly."

"Which of your folks are coming, Yaoyorozu?"

"My mother. It's always her for these sorts of things."

"Mama Yaoyorozu, huh. I'm picturing a really fancy lady!"

The image in Uraraka's mind was basically Momo Yaoyorozu, but scaled and aged up.

"My friends used to say the same thing during my childhood, but to me, she's always just been my mother. It's a lady's duty to keep herself put together while maintaining the household."

A proud sort of smile arose on Yaoyorozu's face, but then her brow crinkled.

"But...she can be a bit of a scatterbrain from time to time..."

"How's that?"

"Mistaking coffee for soy sauce, sugar for salt, or washing her face with toothpaste..."

"The oldest airhead moves in the book!" snorted Uraraka.

"Better than a flawless parent. It's little things like that that really make her feel human."

"I suppose so... Anyhow, who from your family is coming tomorrow, Tsuyu?"

"My dad. You can't miss him, since he'll be the one with the froggy face... Ribbit?"

Asui had picked up on something and was now staring past her classmates.

"What is it?"

"Something about that one guy."

Uraraka and Yaoyorozu turned to spot a thin, fidgety man who was glancing around nervously with hunched shoulders. He looked to be about twenty years old, and he was sweating buckets.

"Maybe he's sick?"

"Then we ought to offer him help before he collapses..."

Yaoyorozu was about to march over and say something when Uraraka gasped.

"Hang on. Isn't that the undies section...?"

Indeed, the man was pacing about the panties corner, surrounded by a bouquet of women's underwear in pink, white, black, beige, purple, and red options. Wary of his clearly suspicious behavior, the three girls hid behind the pajama rack to get a better look.

"A panty thief, maybe...?" murmured a nervous Uraraka.

"Certainly possible," said an anxious Yaoyorozu. "But we mustn't prejudge. Perhaps he's picking out a gift for his significant other...?"

"The panties also might just be for him, Yaoyorozu," said the unflappable Asui.

"Y-yes. I suppose it takes all types…"

Yaoyorozu was shaken but doing her best to maintain composure. Uraraka, meanwhile, was imagining a vast array of hobbies and proclivities.

"Different strokes for different folks, huh…"

"Almost feels like we're the shoplifting police."

"I suspect that no such law enforcement unit exists."

The girls kept observing the man from behind the pajamas. Nobody else around. Uraraka laughed weakly, trying to ignore her nerves.

"Think we're overthinking this? He could just be browsing."

"That's not a normal way to browse, I'd say… But it's true—we can't treat him like a criminal if he hasn't taken anything."

No sooner had the words left Yaoyorozu's mouth than the man stuffed a pair of white panties into his pocket.

"Aha!"

He began to shuffle away from the scene of the crime and the three eyewitnesses.

"H-he really is a thief…"

"M-maybe he'll go pay at the register…?"

"If he walks out now, it's case closed."

While Yaoyorozu and Uraraka shouted in hushed tones—still shocked by what they'd seen—Asui pursued the man silently. Her panicked friends followed. Uraraka prayed that the oddball would veer towards the checkout, but it was in vain. Instead, he made a beeline for the exit and stepped through the automatic doors.

"Yes. He's a thief."

"Stop right there, you!"

The man turned to spot his pursuers, yelped, grew pale, and nearly tripped over himself as he started to bolt.

"We've got a runner!"

"Get back here!"

"Ribbit."

"S-sorry, sorry, sorry!"

Not sorry enough to stop, apparently, but the girls' Hero Course training had paid off, as they soon caught up with him. The man was as good as apprehended when he did something none of them expected.

"What the…?" gasped Uraraka, taken aback as the thin man ripped some flowers out of a nearby planter and began shoveling them into his mouth. A yellow mist shot out of his nose towards the girls, enveloping them.

"What're these yellow particles…?"

"Whatever they are, we'd better not breathe them in… Ribbit…"

"*Koff*, eh…*koff*…"

The trio had gotten a lungful of the stuff, though, and the shoplifter took the opportunity to flee once again.

"Wait, you!"

They started to give chase, but their bodies were already reacting. First, a pang of sluggishness, then itchy eyes and noses. Thinking it must be their imaginations, they kept stumbling after their target.

Itchy eyes. Tickled nostrils. No, *burning* nostrils even.

"S-suddenly not feeling so hot… Achoo!"

"My sinuses… So very itchy! Aahchoo!"

"I think this might be… Ribichoo, ribichoo!"

The sudden symptoms brought the girls to a dead stop, and they turned to look at each other. Bleary red

eyes, running noses, and faces scrunched up in attempts to stave off impending sneezes. All in all, one big mess.

"Was that you sneezing just now, Tsuyu? Too cute."

"Achoo! This is hardly the time for that, Uraraka... These symptoms seem like..."

"Ribbichoo! Like hay fever, yeah..."

"Ah, so maybe that yellow stuff our shoplifter shot out was..."

"Flower pollen, perhaps...? From his Quirk, somehow."

"He can launch pollen after eating flowers...? A-aachoo! Huh?"

During that last sneeze, one of Uraraka's flailing hands had grazed Yaoyorozu, who was now floating away, untethered by gravity.

"Kyaah...?"

"S-sorry, lebbe just... Achoo! Achoo! Achoo! Achoo! Achoo!"

Uraraka attempted to bring her fingertips together to undo the effects, but the barrage of sneezes had her immobilized.

"Achoo! Achoo! Achoo!"

Each of Yaoyorozu's own sneezes propelled her higher and higher, until she was soon level with the tops of the roadside trees.

"I'll geb oo down," croaked a stuffy Asui, launching her frog tongue towards her friend.

"Ribbichoo! Ribbichoo! Ribbichoo!"

Its aim thrown off by the recoil, Asui's tongue instead wrapped around the branches and trunk of a nearby tree, like a great pink python. And still, no end to the sneezing.

"Ribbichoo! Ribbichoo! Ribbichoo!"

"Achoo! Achoo! Achoo! Dangit!"

Yaoyorozu watched her pained classmates struggle to stop sneezing, and though her own nose was still running like mad, she decided to do good by her reputation as the class's biggest brain.

"The solution to hay fever is masks!"

She plucked three flu masks from under her clothes, having created them in an instant with her Quirk.

"Here! Dese should bwock thuh pollen! Achoo!"

"Buh ib's aweady in our systems! Achoooo!"

"Ah, how foolish ob me... Achoo! Achoo!"

Yaoyorozu's wits were no match for the brutal hay fever.

"Achoo... Release!"

Still sneezing, Uraraka managed to bring her hands together and undo her Quirk's effects, sending Yaoyorozu plummeting into the hammock formed by Asui's tangled tongue. Once settled, they helped their friend unwrap her tongue from the tree.

"Thanks... Thought I'd be stuck to that tree forever."

"Of course. It was your tongue that saved me, Tsuyu."

"That hay fever shoplifter won't get away with this!"

Yaoyorozu nodded at the indignant Uraraka.

"No, he won't... Hmm? Are our symptoms clearing up?"

The fierce itchiness and torrent of sneezing seemed to subside.

"Just a passing attack, I guess?"

"We still gotta catch the guy, though."

Sadly, the man was long gone.

"I'm fairly sure he went that way, and he can't have gotten far!"

The allergy attack had lit a fire under the girls, stoking their rage and drive for justice. Their quest led them to a busier street, but their quarry was nowhere in sight. Passersby hadn't spotted him, either.

"Hmm, are we sure he went in this direction?"

"Why don't we ask that woman...? Um, pardon us!"

Ahead stood a clock that seemed perfect for rendezvous, and beneath it was an attractive woman with long hair, glancing around the area.

"Oh? Can I help you?"

"Did you happen to see a young man come past here? One in an obvious panic, perhaps...?"

The woman gave the trio a puzzled look but tried to recall.

"I did see someone. Not really panicking, though."

"It's possible he was acting natural. Trying not to attract attention, maybe," said Asui.

"The guy you saw, was he kinda thin and wimpy looking? About yay high?" asked Uraraka, gesturing.

"No, this one was on the heavier side, and he wore glasses."

"Not our man, then," sighed a disappointed Uraraka.

"I'm sorry I couldn't be more help."

Uraraka shook her head vehemently.

"Nah, we're sorry to have bothered you! We'll catch this hay fever shoplifter yet."

"Catch a what, now...?"

"He's a shoplifter, and his Quirk gives people hay fever! So if you spot a guy with yellow powder shooting out his nose, head for the hills!"

"I will..."

As the girls turned to march away, they didn't notice the young woman's knit brow.

UA

After a bit more searching, they reached a quieter residential area and decided to take a breather in a small park with public restrooms. Despite it being a Sunday afternoon, there wasn't a soul around.

"After all that sneezing, I'd like to freshen up."

"Same. Feeling kinda grimy."

"I'll be washing my stomach, too."

But before they entered the women's restroom,

a man in an obvious hurry dashed in front of them, heading straight for the men's.

"Eh?"

"Ack."

It was their allergy man.

Time seemed to stop for a beat, but then a four-way cry of "Ahhh!" echoed through the park. The man tried to make another break for it.

"Sorry, sorry!"

"If 'sorry' was good enough, we wouldn't need heroes or police, you!"

"We witnessed you stealing the underwear, so surrender yourself at once!"

"Oh no, look…" said Asui with a gasp. Their cornered culprit was making straight for a planter full of flowers. With trembling hands, he yanked out a bunch and spun to face the girls.

"P-please, just let me go!"

"He's threatening to hit us with more hay fever if we approach! How cowardly!"

The threat worked, though, since they were in no hurry to experience that particular torture again.

"There's just…somewhere I've got to get to… I'll

never have this chance again! So please!"

The flowers moved towards the man's mouth, but Yaoyorozu reacted instantly, extracting the flu masks from her pocket.

"Uraraka! Tsuyu! Use these!"

"The masks you made earlier?"

In an instant, all three had donned the masks.

"Keep in mind this is just a stopgap! They won't give us complete protection, so here's what we need to do…"

Yaoyorozu whispered her strategy to the other two, who nodded in turn.

"Okay!"

"Gotcha."

The man had just finished swallowing, but Uraraka's hands were already flying towards the pavement. The affected block of cement floated up, rocking him off-balance and giving Asui the opening she needed to launch her tongue from under her mask and wrap him up tightly. He gave a weak whimper, but in one final act of defiance, he devoured another handful of flowers. The yellow substance streamed from his nose.

"Ack, here comes the pollen!"

"I'm more than prepared for it!" cried Yaoyorozu.

Uraraka and Asui turned to find their friend wielding an oversized *uchiwa* fan that she'd whipped up when they dove into action.

"This should eliminate our pollen problems quite nicely!"

A few strong yet graceful waves of the fan blew the pollen off course, away from the girls.

"Why not an electric fan?" asked Uraraka, mimicking Yaoyorozu's moves with her own hands.

"I don't see a power outlet around, do you? Besides, the Japanese uchiwa is ideal for blowing things away with minimal effort."

"Makes sense!"

With his pollen and escape route gone, the cornered man soon found himself tied up with a length of rope, also courtesy of Yaoyorozu's Creation.

"Back to the store, now!"

"H-hang on a sec!" protested their prisoner, now with his arms seized by Asui and Uraraka.

"You oughta learn when to call it quits," snapped Uraraka.

He pleaded his case.

"At least gimme my one phone call...? There's someone important I can't keep waiting."

"And it's your fault that they're going to keep on waiting! That's what you get for stealing underwear."

"I get that, but..."

Yaoyorozu's reasoned scolding left no room for argument, though, so the man could only hang his head, as pathetic as a puppy abandoned in the rain.

Once everyone had calmed down, Uraraka took on the role of the compassionate seasoned detective.

"Mister, you've got family, yeah? You wanted those panties real bad—I get it, we've all been there—but stealing's just not the way... What would your mother say...?"

"Sorry... I'll return the underwear and... Eh? Panties...?"

Through bleary eyes, the man seemed confused by the accusation.

"Too embarrassed to buy them properly, at the register?" asked Asui, but their prisoner looked just as perplexed.

"W-wait a minute! Who's talking about panties, here?"

"You needn't play dumb. We understand that the

world is full of people with, shall we say, alternative proclivities," said Yaoyorozu with a shake of her head.

"Sometimes you just wanna wear some cute undies, yeah?"

Uraraka was encouraging a confession, but the man wasn't biting.

"W-wrong! I stole a pair of tighty-whities!"

"Is that so?"

Asui plucked the women's underwear from his pocket, and his face went as white as the stolen goods.

"A-all I wanted was some plain old undies for men! Must've panicked and thought those were briefs... Though I usually go with boxers!"

"So it's not some bizarre hobby of yours?" asked Asui, eliciting an almost disappointed groan from Uraraka.

"Regardless, theft is theft."

"Why'd you need underwear so bad?"

With all three pairs of eyes on him, the man mumbled reluctantly.

"I soiled myself..."

"Huh?"

Tears welled up in his eyes.

"There's this girl at college, Miyuki, and for me, it was love at first sight. After four long years of crushing on her, I finally asked her out on a date, and wouldja believe it, she said yes. Been so excited I haven't sleep for three days... My nerves did a number on my stomach this morning, though... Tried to find a bathroom before we met up, but I couldn't, and...I might've had a teeny-tiny accident..."

"Oh..."

Unsure how to react to this confession, the three girls decided to go with some noncommittal nodding.

"Not like I could go on our date with dirty underwear, right? So I tossed them and went to buy a new pair, but...I forgot my wallet..."

"Yikes," said Uraraka, slapping her forehead.

"I was short on time and all outta options, so..."

Yaoyorozu gave him a sympathetic shake of her head.

"Your crime was the byproduct of a series of unfortunate events, then... But I'm afraid that's no justification."

"Why not just go on the date commando style? You've still got pants on, so she'd never know," asked Asui, tilting her head.

"A date with Miyuki without underwear? I could never do that to her!"

As the girls tried to puzzle out the man's romantic rationalizations, a familiar voice came from behind.

"No underwear? I wouldn't have minded."

The long-haired woman from under the clock was standing at the park's entrance.

"M-Miyuki!" shouted the man in shock.

"Eh? *She's* your Miyuki...?"

"Your beloved?"

Uraraka and Yaoyorozu seemed more surprised than the man himself. Asui, less so.

"So you really were after Suzuki. I started wondering, when you mentioned a pollen-shooting shoplifter..." said the woman, approaching the group. Ready to burst into tears, Suzuki tried to run but fell over in a clumsy heap, still bound by Asui's tongue.

"I'm sorry. I overheard everything."

Unsure if they were about to witness a brutal breakup of the young couple, the girls froze—Uraraka flustered, Yaoyorozu nervous, and Asui watching in silence.

"S-sorry, Miyuki! I-I...finally manage to get a date

with you...and I ruin it by crapping myself... Go ahead. Toss me out like yesterday's trash..."

"Underwear or no underwear, soiled or not...you're still you, Suzuki. Always the shrinking violet, not knowing which way's up. I could never abandon a guy like that."

"M-Miyuki..."

Miyuki helped Suzuki up and gave him a warm smile. Now even Asui's eyes were bulging wider than usual in shock at this unexpected turn.

"But stealing's a crime, so you need to go apologize. I'll come with."

"Eh...really?"

"Like I said, someone needs to keep an eye on you."

"Oh, Miyuki!

A complete turnabout. Somehow or other, love was still in the air.

After thanking the high school girls, the couple left for the supermarket. Only once they were out of sight did Uraraka and Yaoyorozu release a pair of pent-up sighs.

"That was...exhausting!"

"Yes. Emotionally, even..."

"We caught the shoplifter, and his love life's gonna be okay. Things could be worse," said a nonchalant Asui.

"All's well that ends well, yeah? Honestly, that pitiful guy and his on-point lady seem like a match made in heaven."

"There's something I don't understand, though."

"What's that?"

"Miyuki's reaction. Wouldn't she want her boyfriend to be a bit bolder? I mean, first he soils himself, and then his solution was to steal? I would expect her to become disillusioned with him, and yet..."

Yaoyorozu shook her head in confusion, but Uraraka recalled the first time she'd met Midoriya.

"I get the whole not-abandoning-him thing. She's just worried."

His mop of hair. His giant backpack. His legs trembling, almost comically. Something about Midoriya's not-quite-there-but-can-do attitude had put Uraraka at ease that day, so when he'd tripped, she had instinctively reached out. Since then, it had mostly been him doing the saving.

"Why the smile, Ochaco? Remembering something funny?"

She dropped her cheeks, which must've floated up into a smile all on their own.

"Nah, nothing. But I bet there're plenty of girls who have a thing for fixer-uppers. Ones who like a guy with some minor issues."

"Sure. It takes all types."

"I wonder, could I ever love a man who soils himself...?" asked an uneasy Yaoyorozu, raising her hands to her cheeks.

Ever the levelheaded one, Asui responded. "I say toss the dirty underwear."

"Or just, y'know, wash them?" said Uraraka flatly. Yaoyorozu's face crinkled.

"I'm not speaking of the actual underwear..."

Suddenly, a grumble from Uraraka's stomach.

"All that running worked up an appetite... Ah! My mochi!" she shouted, remembering the shopping cart they'd left near the pajama rack.

"Totally slipped my mind. Let's hope your mochi's still sitting there..."

"Shall we go back and check?"

"Yeah."

"Actually, I'd be willing to try your chocolate mochi concoction at this point."

"We'll make it happen!"

With visions of mochi dancing in their heads, the trio started running back to the supermarket, none the wiser to the challenges the very next day would bring.

Part 6
1-A: Parents' Day

The day had arrived.

Izuku Midoriya entered the 1-A classroom to find Ochaco Uraraka in an animated conversation with her neighbor, Tsuyu Asui.

"And today I'm having curry mochi, so... Oh! Morning, Deku."

"Good morning, Midoriya."

"Uraraka, Tsuyu, good morning."

The boy couldn't help but blush at the sight of Uraraka's quintessentially Uraraka smile. He still had a little trouble talking to girls, though he'd already come a long way in that department.

"So, it's Parents' Day. Who's coming to see you, Deku?"

"My mom. She seemed a little nervous, actually."

"Oh yeah? My dad did too!"

"Must be contagious," said Midoriya, forcing a smile. He left the girls and headed for the back of the classroom, to his seat by the window. The room itself was the same as ever, but everything felt strangely on edge. The students of 1-A couldn't stop chattering about what their families were like and who would be coming.

Guess everyone else feels a little awkward about Parents' Day too.

Parents, visiting one's school? There was always such a clear division between those two realms, so to Midoriya, smashing them together felt decidedly unreal. Embarrassed or not, though, he didn't hate the idea of his mom showing up; in a way, he felt proud. And he wasn't the only student who wanted a parent to see them flourishing at the school of their dreams.

But we gotta read those letters, ugh…

He'd written his after getting home from the hero exhibit the day before. The letter was peppered with permutations of "I'm working hard" and "Sorry to worry you all the time" and had proven a challenge, in

the end. Still, it was honest. Honest enough to make it embarrassing.

A subtle sigh escaped Midoriya's lips.

"What's wrong?"

"Oh. Morning, Todoroki."

"Mhm."

Shoto Todoroki's almost pained stare made Midoriya realize his friend was still waiting for an answer.

"O-oh, nothing wrong really. Just feeling embarrassed in advance about reading my letter."

"Uh-huh."

Only natural that everyone felt the same way, Midoriya thought.

"You write yours, Todoroki?"

"Yeah. For my sister, actually."

"Your big sister's coming today?"

"Mhm."

"Oh."

Just as Midoriya managed a smile at Todoroki's curt answers, Tenya Ida interrupted his own conversation with Fumikage Tokoyami to chime in, and Minoru Mineta and Denki Kaminari joined.

"Good morning, Midoriya! And a happy Parents' Day to you!"

"Morning... Ah, how was the theme park yester-day? Sorry again that I couldn't make it!" said Midoriya, suddenly remembering his friend's Sunday plans. Ida smiled and shook his head vigorously.

"Think nothing of it. Our day was anything but ordinary, though we thoroughly enjoyed ourselves. Wouldn't you agree, Tokoyami?"

"Sure..."

The bird-headed boy forced a nod, but Mineta had more to say on the matter.

"Get this, Midoriya! Tokoyami is a cradle robber!"

"Ehh?"

"What? Enough of your falsehoods!"

Kaminari gave a weak laugh at Midoriya's shock and explained.

"Nah, not really. But a little kid did confess her love for Tokoyami."

"Why, though?"

"It's far too long a story to recount at the moment, and none among us can predict where it may lead, but suffice it to say, no cradles have been pilfered by our good Tokoyami."

Mineta took issue with Ida's clarification.

"Who can say, though, once she grows up! If he was smart, he'd raise her to be his ideal bride, just like old Hikaru Genji did with Princess Akashi!"

Tokoyami glared at Mineta with utter contempt.

"You're the only one who would enact such a scheme."

"Would if I could! Cuz there's nothing illegal about it!"

"They should make your existence illegal, Mineta."

The barb came from Kyoka Jiro, who had been talking with Momo Yaoyorozu but was sickened by Mineta's unconstrained lust this early in the morning. A pair of stretchy cords hung from her earlobes. Her Quirk, "Earphone Jack," allowed her to jack in and amplify the sound waves of her own heartbeat.

"Flatties don't get a say in this," quipped Mineta with scorn.

"Huhh?!"

Jiro looked ready to murder him, but Ida tilted his head in confusion.

"Flatties? What does that mean?"

"Small boobs, man."

"Don't actually tell him, Kaminari! And stop asking

about these things, Ida!"

"How rude. Breasts are breasts, and one shouldn't get hung up on their relative size."

Yaoyorozu nodded, agreeing with Ida.

"He's quite right, Jiro."

"Hard to take that to heart, coming from you, Yaoyorozu," said Jiro, hinting at her friend's extraordinary bosom.

"Anyhow, as I was saying, the chocolate mochi was better than I expected!"

"Seriously?"

Chocolate mochi...?

Midoriya finally reached his seat, but his classmates' bizarre conversations had already given him plenty to wonder about. The day's shortened homeroom was about to begin, and Aizawa was sure to arrive just on time.

But he didn't.

The disciplined students were plenty used to planting themselves in their seats in time, so they took note when the bell chimed and their teacher didn't slink through the door.

"Aizawa Sensei's not here?" asked Toru Hagakure,

from her seat in the front row.

"Ribbit? Just late, maybe?"

"A U.A. educator, late on an exhibition day! Why, a situation this dire could shake the very foundations of our school!" shouted Ida, shooting to his feet and swinging his arms like a steam locomotive's wheels. Hanta Sero, the slim boy seated in front of Tokoyami, tried to calm the panicking president.

"C'mon, even Aizawa Sensei's just human. Everyone's late from time to time."

"But, Sero! Heroes are locked in an eternal battle against the ticking clock! It can mean life or death for those needing to be saved, so even a single second of tardiness is a grave sin!"

Midoriya thought to himself as he watched Ida's outburst, *It is weird. Aizawa Sensei's never late...*

Even after suffering nearly disfiguring injuries during the villain attack on U.S.J., Aizawa had shown up in the classroom wrapped in bandages, as if it were business as usual.

"I hope nothing happened to him..."

"Quit yer muttering, dammit," shot back Katsuki Bakugo from his seat in front of Midoriya's, not even bothering to turn around.

"Sorry, Kacchan, but honestly…"

But Bakugo stayed facing forward, with zero interest in whatever Midoriya had to say.

So he's a little late. Let's not make a mountain out of a molehill, right? I bet he'll show up in a minute.

The bell rang to mark the end of homeroom, but still no Aizawa. Definitely odd. The chattering intensified, and Yaoyorozu wondered out loud, "Isn't it nearly time for our parents to arrive as well?"

"Yeah. Not just yet, but pretty soon, anyway…" said Eijiro Kirishima, the eternal optimist who sat next to Sero. Yaoyorozu's brow crinkled.

"But we haven't seen a single one…"

"Maybe they got lost?" said Jiro.

Mina Ashido, a girl with black eyes, pinkish-purple hair and skin, and a pair of antennae sprouting from her head, chimed in.

"Yeah, cuz U.A.'s huge, remember?" she said with her trademark Pollyanna smile.

"Attention, all. As class president, I will travel to the staff room to check. Please wait here until I return."

But before Ida could make it to the door, everyone's

phones buzzed in unison.

"Hmm?"

Midoriya checked his phone in a panic.

"A message from Aizawa Sensei!"

It read, RIDE BUS TO MOCK CITYSCAPE. NOW. He was referring to the training grounds constructed to resemble a built-up downtown zone. With neighborhoods alpha through sigma, the grounds were as large as a real city and had been the site of the entrance exam's practical portion.

"The cityscape? But why…?"

As if a light bulb had sparked over his head, Kaminari said, "I've got it! Aizawa Sensei probably wants to hold the model class, the letter reading, and the facility tour all in one place! It's only 'rational'!"

Everyone agreed that that did sound like their teacher, so they reluctantly started to move.

"It doesn't seem we have a choice… Be sure not to forget your letters!"

Ida led the class to the parking lot, where they found and boarded a bus waiting for them—one of several used to shuttle U.A. students around the massive campus.

"Why not just have us meet there in the first place? This sucks," grumbled Mineta. To his right, Midoriya responded with a noncommittal chuckle before settling into deep, puzzled thought.

"What is it, Midoriya?" asked Ida from the neighboring seat.

"It's just… Making us waste time like this? Does that sound like Aizawa Sensei?"

"No, it does not. I quite agree," replied Ida, his eyes blinking rapidly.

On Ida's right, Todoroki listened in silence, knowing that everything their rational teacher did, he did for a reason.

"Stop overthinking it, Midoriya! You're gonna go bald early, at this rate! So Aizawa screwed up? So what?"

"Harsh!" snorted Uraraka from across the aisle. Asui, sitting next to her, spoke up.

"Would you dare say that to Aizawa Sensei's face, Mineta?"

"Course I wouldn't, so you'd better not rat me out!" Ida gasped.

"Perhaps this is all intentional on Sensei's part!"

"How's that?"

"For heroes, the call to action can arrive at any moment. This could be an exercise designed to test our reactions."

"Yeah, that's possible," added Todoroki, who noticed Ida yawning. "Tired? That's not like you."

"Apologies, something about rattling vehicles does this to me... Plus, I was up all night paring down my too-long letter from forty pages to twenty."

"And you still wound up with twenty whole pages?!"

Ida nodded at the shocked Midoriya.

"I couldn't bear to eliminate another word... Not when every last one is filled with my deepest gratitude!"

"That explains the bulge in your bucket."

Todoroki wasn't wrong—the pocket that held Ida's letter was stuffed to bursting. He took out the fat envelope, prompting Uraraka to say, "Sure wish my wallet had that kinda paper in it."

Midoriya couldn't help but return her beaming smile with one of his own.

Probably overthinking this. Yeah.

He took a look at his own letter, which—though not as lengthy as Ida's—was clearly written with care.

Hope you brought a hankie, Mom.

What he'd written probably wouldn't come across as all too moving to anyone else, but his mother was prone to waterworks. At that moment, Midoriya couldn't have known that the scene he imagined would never come to pass.

U𝖠

The bus dropped the class at the mock cityscape and sped off. Aizawa was nowhere to be found.

"Sensei must be farther inside. Let's move, everyone!" commanded Ida with a raised arm, but Mezo Shoji—an enormous boy with extra noses on the tips of his tentacles—said, "Wait. I smell something." His Quirk was "Dupli-Arms," and he could spawn copies of his body parts on a set of extra appendages, all connected by winglike membranes.

"D-don't lookit me!" protested Mineta.

"Not you… Smells like gasoline."

"Maybe there's a fake pileup in there, for training purp—"

Kaminari's thought was cut short by a scream in the distance.

"What the?"

A series of cries joined the scream.

The students broke into a run towards the voices, which led them to a street lined with buildings. Midoriya's sneaking suspicions from the bus returned in full force as the smell of gasoline grew stronger.

"What's going on over there...?" muttered a dumbfounded Kirishima, grinding to a halt. Before them lay a cleared lot, with the buildings that had occupied the space smashed to craggy piles of rubble on either side. In the middle—a massive pit, around twenty meters in diameter. At the very center, a large cubic cage seemed to float on a small platform in midair, but it was actually balanced on a slender tower, like an apple core nearly eaten clean away. The muddled screams from a moment before now came across loud and clear.

"Ochaco!"

"Dad?!"

"Shoto..."

"Huh...?""""

"Tenya!"

"Mother!"

"Izuku!"

"M-Mom, is that you...?" gasped Midoriya, spotting his mother in her navy blue outfit.

Yes, it was their parents locked up in the cage, shouting in terror for their children, who quickly scampered to the very edge of the pit.

"Yech... It really is gasoline...?"

Uraraka peered down to discover a layer of stagnant liquid eight to nine meters below.

"What the heck happened? How'd our parents get in there...?"

"And where's Aizawa Sensei in all this?"

A cool, mechanical voice rang out to answer the panicked students' questions.

"Aizawa is down for a nap. A nice *dirt nap*."

Despite the artificial-sounding tone, the words were somehow filled with malice. Midoriya and the others braced themselves.

"A dirt nap...?"

"You saying Aizawa Sensei's *dead*...?"

"Can't be! I mean, har har, but April Fools' Day was a while back! So show yourself, whoever you are!"

"Calm yourselves. You are free to think this is a joke, but be aware that there are hostages in play."

"Hostages...?"

Midoriya's brain struggled to keep up with the sudden crisis, and he—along with Ida and Todoroki—found himself scanning the area for the hostile entity.

"No. Not here. The voice is coming from inside the cage," said Shoji, whose tentacles had sprouted extra ears.

"Inside the...?"

"Correct. I am in here with them."

As if on cue, the group of parents flinched away from the back of the cage, where a dark figure now appeared. A tall man, wearing a black mask, cape, and cowl. The parents scurried into the corners of their prison.

Midoriya's entire body went rigid.

Why? How? Who could've...

Seizing the moment, Ida pulled out his phone and began to make a call.

"I should mention now that contacting your school

or the authorities is not permitted. Ah, and I'm afraid that little Denki's Quirk cannot help you either," said the figure, addressing Kaminari.

"What the hell, man...?"

So he knows all about us somehow...?

The man went on.

"Fleeing or seeking outside help is also forbidden. Attempt to run, and it will be your parent who pays the price."

At that, a well-built, genial-looking man rattled the bars of the cage and shouted.

"Dangit! Can't do a thing about these solid bars!"

"D-Dad!" cried Uraraka from the edge of the pit, feeling utterly helpless.

"H-help us, Momo!"

"You mustn't panic, Mother... Keep calm..."

Already in a state of shock, Yaoyorozu was further shaken by her typically composed mother's panic. Beside Mrs. Yaoyorozu stood a man in a suit—Asui's father.

"*Croak, croak.*"

"That croak means danger... Ribbit..."

Asui was the most levelheaded of them all, so the

note of distress in her voice only made matters worse. Their teacher, dead? Their parents, hostages? None of it felt real.

"Mom…"

Seeing his mother weeping in the cage, Midoriya felt the blood drain from his face.

"Why… Why's this happening…?"

The man spoke again.

"I flunked out of U.A. High. Gaining entry in the hopes of becoming a hero was all I ever had. That an excellent specimen such as myself failed is proof enough that this world is cruel and misaligned. Imagine that. Me, a dropout? However, if left to your own devices, only the brightest of futures await you children. That is why I've—"

"So you put on that stupid black cape just to throw a little tantrum, you dumbass?" screamed Bakugo.

"Kacchan!"

"I'm already bored. Let's blow this guy to kingdom come!"

Bakugo's indomitable grin was accompanied by a small explosion in his palm. He dashed to the edge, about to let his fiery momentum carry him straight to the central platform.

"Slow down. Or have you already forgotten about the hostages?"

With that, the man dragged the nearest woman towards himself. It was Mitsuki Bakugo. Her son clucked his tongue and skidded to a halt. From experience, Midoriya knew what panic looked like on Bakugo's face, and it was there now.

"Great job getting yourself caught, hag!"

His mother went from abject fear to rage, just like that.

"I've told you a million times not to call me 'hag,' you little punk!"

The unexpected roar from Mitsuki drew all eyes to her in vacant shock.

"Wow. I, uh, see the family resemblance."

"That s'posed to be a compliment, broomhead?" snapped Bakugo at the dumbstruck Kirishima.

Inside the cage, Inko Midoriya spoke to Mitsuki in troubled tones.

"Mrs. Bakugo, please, we're hostages, remember...?"

"Oh, whoops! True enough!"

"Pipe down," said the man, releasing Bakugo's mother and shoving her aside.

"That woman has nerves of steel..."

"Yeah, she's one tough lady, same as ever..."

Midoriya answered Ida with a pained smile.

This was the woman who'd raised that pint-sized general, and she was never one to let her own bossy son push her around. Midoriya could remember a few times when he'd gotten a tongue-lashing from Mitsuki for his involvement in Bakugo's antics.

Feeling a little more collected now, thanks to her. Phew. What I... What we need to do now is save the hostages. So first...

"What are you after, here?" asked Midoriya in a calm, commanding voice, eyes locked on the villain.

"What am I after? One thing only—the utter destruction of you golden children and your bright futures. And slaughtering your parents while you watch is just the way to do it."

"All this, just to get to us?" came a quivering shout from Mashirao Ojiro, a boy whose Quirk equipped him with a thick tail. Beside him, Kirishima raged.

"You got a beef with us? Then bring it! But leave

our folks outta this!"

"Oh, but it isn't your bodies I aim to destroy. No. It will be that much more painful when your parents suffer and you would-be heroes have nobody but yourselves to blame," said the man with what must have been a sneer under his mask.

"If you truly walked the path of the hero once, then stop this foolishness!" screamed Yaoyorozu, unable to contain herself. Ashido backed her up.

"Exactly! And you're headed for the slammer when all's said and done!"

"Oh, I have no intention of escaping. After all, I have nothing left to lose. So for my final act, I might as well savor your descent into agony as you watch your parents perish. Now, who to start with...?"

The villain reached towards the hostages, who shrank into the corner of the cage.

"Quit it!"

Inspired by Uraraka's desperate cry, Midoriya plunged into thought.

Getting our parents outta there means doing something about the villain, first. But dealing with him means we need a way to shield the hostages...

"...But it's not like we can free them without him noticing... The cage is too exposed. No blind angles... Plus, it's about ten meters to the platform, across the pit. He's sure to spot us making a move... Darn. I've got nothing."

"Keep it down, Midoriya. He'll hear," said Todoroki at the front of the pack, not wanting the villain to overhear Midoriya's usual muttered monologue.

"Ah, sorry. Couldn't help it..."

"No ideas then, Midoriya?" whispered Ida, standing near Todoroki.

"No, not yet..."

"Very well... Everyone, we need to distract this villain somehow."

"Gotcha. We'll get the job done."

"And you think up a plan. Quick."

Kirishima and Kaminari stepped forward at Ida's call to action. A few others followed, ready to keep the villain's attention occupied.

"Stand back, friends. We need a distraction, *non*? Such is my expertise. ☆"

Yuga Aoyama shot the group a sparkling, pretentious wink and practically pirouetted forward.

"This unsightly crime simply won't do. ☆ Besides, who could possibly commit such evil while looking upon my beautiful visage? Wouldn't you agree, Koda?"

"Oh, um, well... Uh-huh."

Koji Koda's large, rocky body seemed to shrink at Aoyama's prompt.

"Why involve soft-spoken Koda?" protested Ida under his breath.

Throwing his friend a lifeline, Rikido Sato added, "Don't mess with Koda like that!"

In a sense, Aoyama's distraction was working.

"C'mon, guys, don't..." muttered Midoriya without thinking, but Todoroki interrupted.

"They all know we're in a tight spot. Our only chance is a sneak attack from *you*."

"You think?"

"You're good at that. Smashing the unsmashable, and all that."

Midoriya felt tears welling up, but he gritted his teeth and started thinking. No time for crying. Not when their families' lives were at stake.

Sneak attack... Right. Head-on won't work. Get the drop on him and pin him down, if only for a second.

Enough time for Ida and Kacchan to get over there. Just a second or two...

Then it came to him.

Of course. If it's all about sneaking, we need...

Midoriya called over Hagakure, Yaoyorozu, and Uraraka.

"A stun gun?"

"Mhm. Small enough to stay under the radar, but with plenty of oomph. Can you whip that up?"

"Excellent idea. And yes, I can," said Yaoyorozu with a nod. A pocket-sized device emerged from her palm, and she handed it to Uraraka.

"I made it brown so he's less likely to notice."

"Now I just gotta make this thing and Hagakure float?" asked Uraraka.

"Yup. Since Hagakure's the perfect candidate."

"Just a sec! Lemme strip down, in that case."

True to her word, the invisible girl's clothes fell to ground, prompting a frantic "Whaaat?" from behind Midoriya.

"Hoo boy! A babe in the nude! Invisible or not, my brain's filling in the details just fine!"

Mineta was meant to be part of the distraction crew,

but now he barged his way over to the mission team. Asui's frog tongue shot towards him.

"No self-control, even in an emergency, Mineta?" she said, slamming him to the ground.

"Bwahh!"

As Midoriya gave Mineta a strange look, he felt a tap on his shoulder. Nobody there, except the invisible Hagakure.

"I'm ready to do this, 'kay?"

"Be careful, Hagakure..."

"You can count on me!"

A light touch from Uraraka sent the tiny stun gun and its wielder floating towards the cage. Rather than point it out, the distraction crew ramped up their act.

Please... Let this work!

Midoriya joined the rest of the class while keeping a close eye on the target. The man in black was nearly at his wit's end when the weapon landed near him, outside the cage. Hagakure must've been crouching, as the stun gun seemed to snake along the ground.

"I said, silence. Do not make me repeat myself!" snapped the villain, now pacing about the cage.

Almost there, almost there!

As if obeying Midoriya's thoughts, the stun gun settled just outside the bars. Now it was a matter of timing.

"Perhaps the most boisterous child's parent should be the first to die? Then you lot might see things differently…"

He stopped pacing to survey the group of parents, and the electrified weapon hovered between the bars, inching towards his leg, crackling and sparking. But before it could connect, the villain deftly whipped around, kicking the stun gun into the pit.

"Ack!"

"It seems an invisible pest has wormed its way over here!"

Shaking with rage, he threw open the cage door, stepped out, and drew a lighter from inside his cape.

"I had hoped to serve up individual doses of suffering, but no matter. We will all dine in hell together."

"Don't do it!"

But Midoriya's cry fell on deaf ears. The villain tossed the lighter into the pit, transforming it into a raging inferno.

"No!"

He swallowed a blast of hot air, and the instant heat singed his cheeks. Beyond the dancing flames, Midoriya could see his classmates' parents, deep in despair, yet enduring.

"Izuku!"

"Mom!"

The boy's mother shouted for help, extending her hand from within the cage, and Midoriya reached out instinctively. Wind fanned the flames even higher, and Inko vanished from view.

"This is all my fault…"

His strategy had failed.

Everyone was counting on me!

On the verge of despair, Midoriya started to collapse, and a kick from behind finished the job.

"Huh…?"

"You really that stupid?"

Midoriya regained his balance and turned to find Bakugo wearing a grim expression that turned into a vicious smile as he eyed the villain.

"This is the perfect chance, dumbass!"

"Kacchan?"

"Hey, roundface!" Bakugo spat at Uraraka. "Get me floating!"

The girl did as commanded, and Bakugo rocketed towards the villain. Midoriya gasped. Of course—the man was outside of the cage.

Todoroki shot a blast of ice, which Bakugo dodged in midair with lightning reflexes.

"Watch it, you half 'n' half bastard!"

The ice found the villain's feet, freezing him to the ground.

"Tch!"

"You like wearing black? Try black and blue!"

Bakugo straddled the villain, threatening him with explosions from his palm.

"Let us join him!"

Ida's cry got Midoriya to his feet, and with a touch from Uraraka, he was off.

"Thanks!"

"Help my dad out, 'kay…?"

Midoriya nodded at the panicked girl, uncertain if there was anything reassuring about his smile.

Gotta picture the power flowing through my whole body…

One For All, the Quirk granted to him by All Might, surged through his blood, muscles, and cells, and Midoriya leaped into the air beside Ida. Tokoyami and Todoroki jumped after them, while the latter continued his icy assault. The roaring flames from the pit singed Midoriya as he flew, but he landed on the platform and ran to his mother.

"Izuku!"

"You okay, Mom?"

She nodded, and Midoriya rushed over to Bakugo.

"Kacchan!"

The boy had the villain pinned to the ground, keeping him in check with small explosions.

"This shit-eating punk's not so tough. Got him handled, all on my own."

"Katsuki, don't say 'shit'!"

"Stuff it, you shitty hag!"

Mitsuki Bakugo, now out of the cage, put any celebration aside to tear into her son. Midoriya forced a weak smile at the bickering duo before noticing that the villain had pulled out a small something from within his cape.

"Wait, that's…" gasped Midoriya, but he was too

late. The villain's thumb came down with a click. An explosion from below. The apple-core tower supporting the cage began to sway.

"What...?!"

"What'd you do, dammit?" demanded Bakugo.

"As I said, the gates of hell await us all."

The bomb trigger rolled from his open hand.

"The fiend planted explosives in advance...? Whoa!" said Ida, rocked off-balance by the shifting platform. Back at the edge of the pit, Ojiro shouted to the rescue team.

"Hey! The base is crumbling! You guys gotta get back here quick!"

Uraraka and the others were busy using fire extinguishers provided by Yaoyorozu, but their efforts were in vain.

"Dangit! We'll never kill these flames in time..."

"Rather than extinguish the inferno, perhaps a more rational solution... Ah, I've got it!"

Screams from the parents rose as the ground beneath them started to tilt. Before the platform and cage could collapse into the sea of flames, though, Todoroki launched a tendril of ice that latched on to the pit's outer edge, keeping the tower upright for the time being. But like ice cream in a heat wave, the icy bridge started melting straightaway.

"Ladies first! Please grab ahold of me!" shouted Ida.

"B-but…"

The apple-core tower gave another shudder, and the leaping flames threatened to engulf the entire platform. Within the group of huddled parents, Inko Midoriya seemed ready to cry.

"Izuku…"

What kind of hero can't protect his own loved ones…?

He forced his face into a trembling smile.

"It'll be all right. I'm here to save you."

"Oh, Izuku…"

Think, think, think. Evacuating one at a time? No… Need to get everyone away all at once.

Todoroki's voice rang out.

"Damn… Whatever you do, do it soon!"

The boy kept the ice flowing in an attempt to thicken the bridge, but it melted away just as quickly.

"Ice bridge… Slipping… Sliding…? That's it… A slide!" gasped Midoriya.

"Stop joking around, Midoriya! There's no time!"

"A slide, Ida! Like from our rescue training!"

"The evacuation chute?"

Todoroki caught on.

"Right! Just need a way to slide everyone across my ice bridge!"

"I dunno if there's enough time for Yaoyorozu to create a tarp that big, though."

"It's nearly ready, actually!"

At the pit's edge, a massive tarp burst from Yaoyorozu's back, ripping through her shirt.

"I've been working on this fireproof sheet since a few moments ago. Uraraka, Sero, it's your turn!"

"Okay!"

"Here we go!"

Uraraka gave the tarp her magic touch and passed it to Sero, who, courtesy of his "Tape" Quirk, launched it across the pit with the sticky tape that shot from his elbows.

"Grab it, Dark Shadow!"

"Aye, aye!"

With tape trailing behind it, the tarp landed in the clutches of Dark Shadow, who passed it to Midoriya.

"Thanks! Should've known you'd be on top of things,

Yaoyorozu!" said Midoriya, spreading the tarp out.

"Everyone, please climb aboard!"

With the ground swaying more by the second, the parents wasted no time in following Midoriya's orders.

"You here with us, Hagakure?"

"Sure am!"

"Ida, use your Engine to pull from the front, while the rest of us push from behind. And you keep blasting your ice until the last second, Todoroki."

"Got it."

"What about the villain?" asked Tokoyami. Bakugo yanked the man to his feet; all the fight seemed to have left him.

"We can't just leave him here."

"Any funny business, and you go boom, get it?"

The ground heaved.

"Here I go, Midoriya!"

Ida took the lead, grabbing the front corners of the tarp with arms stretched behind him.

"Go, go!"

"No holding back… Torque Over, Reciproburst!"

A pair of explosions and streams of sooty smoke shot from the engines on Ida's calves as he kicked off.

His power-packed ultimate move would stall his engines after a single use, but it was sure to give him the torque and speed he needed in a pinch.

"Urgh!"

Midoriya, Tokoyami, and Bakugo pushed from behind, eager to match Ida's contribution, and even Dark Shadow helped, lifting the rear corners of the tarp. Todoroki leaped on at the last second.

The group flew across the ice bridge like a runaway freight train, dragged forward by Ida's gale-force speed. His feet reached the edge of the pit before the parents even had a chance to scream.

"All righ—whoa!"

Uraraka's prayers were answered, but her victory cry was cut short by a crash as the tower collapsed into the fire. The ice bridge plummeted, leaving Midoriya and the other rear guard members to dangle from the hanging edge of the tarp, without a foothold.

"Yikes!"

The pages of Midoriya's letter fluttered from his pocket into the hungry flames below.

"Urk!"

Sensing that the entire tarp might be dragged over

the edge, Ida braced himself, while Uraraka and the others hurried over to help pull.

"One, two, three!"

They yanked the tarp up before the flames could consume it. The jolt, however, loosened Inko Midoriya's sweaty grip. She was airborne.

"Ahhh!"

"Mom, no!"

In a flash, the black-garbed villain had her in one arm, with the other gripping the edge. Only Midoriya and his mother realized what had happened, since the entire group was back on solid ground within seconds.

"She's safe..." muttered Midoriya as his mother scampered over to him.

"Are you okay, Izuku...?"

"Yeah. Just glad you are too, Mom..."

She wept and embraced her son, but he could only grimace.

Went and made her worry again...

Then he remembered the villain.

"Where'd he go...?"

The man in black stood apart from the group and spoke.

"Congratulations. The exercise is over."

"Huh? What's that mean...?"

"Somebody grab him. We gotta contact the school!"

"And find where he stashed Aizawa Sensei..."

Blood drained from the students' faces, but before they could lament the loss of their teacher, a familiar listless voice rang out.

"Me? I'm right here."

It was Aizawa, emerging from the shadows of the nearby rubble.

"Huh?"

Their eyes popped. While the students of 1-A tried to digest this revelation, Aizawa approached the group of parents as nonchalantly as if they hadn't just raced across a sea of fire.

"Excellent work, everyone. Quite the convincing performance."

"You're making me blush! It's all thanks to your coaching, Sensei!" said Uraraka's father, beaming.

Nearby, Yaoyorozu's mother sighed, glad to be done with her duty.

"That was nerve-racking, I daresay."

Asui's father was speaking with Mitsuki Bakugo.

"Didn't know what to think when you almost broke character, Mrs. Bakugo. *Croak*."

"So sorry! Couldn't help it…"

Cowering in fear one minute, chatting like old friends the next. Aizawa turned to his dumbfounded class.

"Still don't get it? Let me spell it out: this was all a setup."

Their "Huhh?!" in unison echoed throughout the mock cityscape.

"Th-the villain, too…?"

"Yes… We hired an actor from a theater troupe."

"A what, now…? Oh, indeed. Apologies for menacing you kids the way I did!"

The man in black tilted his head almost sheepishly, eliciting a "What the heck?" from a drained Kaminari. Bakugo clucked his tongue.

"No wonder the mook went down so easy. Just some backup player, huh."

"Now just a minute! Wasn't this a bit much...? One wrong move, and somebody could have gotten terribly hurt, or worse!"

Yaoyorozu felt compelled to protest, but Aizawa's answer was as blasé as ever.

"We were prepared for the worst, so no, it wasn't a 'bit much.' Besides, pros are no strangers to danger, so an exercise with lower stakes wouldn't do you much good."

"I suppose that's true..."

Aizawa stared at the girl and spoke again, slowly.

"Were you scared? Scared for your mother?"

"Yes. Quite," came her meek answer.

"Words alone can't express your love for your families. When faced with losing them, however... This provided that valuable experience."

He glanced from student to student.

"A proper rescue demands strength, skill, knowledge, and decisiveness, but emotion can easily cloud judgment. Anyone hoping to become a hero can't very well be flustered by a family member in danger. This exercise, under the guise of 'Parents' Day,' was meant to teach you all just that."

"Yes, Sensei," said Yaoyorozu with a nod. Midoriya understood too.

"One more thing. It's not just about keeping a level head. The people you aim to save—their lives are more than just their own, as they too have families waiting for them to come home. Take that to heart."

A humble chorus of "Yes, Sensei" arose from the students.

"Now, though every hostage was rescued, this could've gone better."

"Huh?"

"You struggled far too much against this single opponent. Wasted too much time. And the stun gun? Hardly the most rational option. Choosing to distract the villain by *talking* to him was an unrefined approach, and it meant putting your eggs in one basket. I've got plenty more to say, but for now... You all passed. By a slim margin."

The sense of relief from the class was visible.

"I want one page on what you've learned from this, due tomorrow."

Amidst the instant wave of grumbles, Ida's hand shot up.

"And what of our letters of appreciation…? Another of your 'rational deceptions' to disguise the true intent of this exercise, Sensei?"

"Well, didn't writing that letter get you thinking about your family more than usual?"

"Indeed, it did!"

The dogged Ida was instantly persuaded, and the end-of-period bell rang out.

"We're done for today. Parents—thank you all for your assistance."

The parents returned Aizawa's bow, and each student drifted towards his or her mother or father.

"Tenya, that final dash was incredible."

"Only thanks to the orange juice you squeezed for me this morning, Mother," replied a proud Ida. Nearby, Uraraka's father gave her a pat on the back.

"You good, Ochaco?"

"Relieved, mostly…blegh!"

"You did great, honey!"

"Thanks!"

Meanwhile, the Bakugos engaged in a war of words.

"Why's your mouth so goddamned foul, boy?"

"Learned from the best, hag!"

"I got it from you, though!"

At a distance, Fuyumi spoke to her little brother.

"We're lucky it was me here at Parents' Day... Mom might've fainted right off the bat, having to play a hostage."

"Yeah. Probably."

"Excuse me, miss."

Aizawa approached, and Fuyumi gave him a small bow.

"Here at U.A., most of our Basic Hero Training classes are recorded, and this one was no exception. If you want, I could give your brother a copy of the footage tomorrow."

"Could you, really?"

"Mhm. There's no harm in having the rest of your family view it."

"Thank you so much," said Fuyumi, bowing again as Aizawa walked away.

"He must've realized that I wanted Mom to see it. You'll have to thank him later, Shoto."

"Sure."

"You know Mom's gonna be thrilled."

"Uh-huh."

Some of the tension left Todoroki's face. A few paces away, Inko Midoriya apologized to her son.

"I'm sorry I couldn't tell you! Your teacher said it was all part of a larger lesson, so I only wanted to help, however possible."

"It's okay, Mom. Really," said Midoriya with a shake of his head. He glanced at her navy blue outfit and noticed it was caked with dirt and soot.

That's why she mentioned it getting stained. Boy, can't believe I didn't pick up on that.

He sighed, a little disappointed with himself.

"But when you said, 'I'm here to save you,' you were the spitting image of a real hero!" said Inko with a wide smile and tear-filled eyes. Midoriya felt a powerful warmth welling up within.

Maybe I actually managed to be reassuring…?

His embarrassment, joy, and pride coalesced into a smile of his own, but then he remembered his letter, now burned to cinders.

Letter or no letter, I've gotta try to tell her.

"So, um, sorry that I'm always making you worry, but I gotta keep trying… Harder and harder…"

"Of course. And your mom's watching over you."

Her eyes filled up with a fresh batch of tears, and Midoriya knew that behind her smile and reassurance lay concern and fear.

"Thanks," he said, holding back his own tears.

"How about some nice *katsudon* tonight?"

"Sure!"

Once the entire group began walking back to the bus stop, Inko noticed the man in black, who was keeping his distance.

"Oh, I really must say something to him, too!"

She walked over to the faux villain, bowed, and said, "I have to thank you for back there!"

"Nonsense, ma'am. I only did what came naturally! Thank goodness you made it out in one piece!"

Midoriya squinted up at the man.

"What is it, kid? Something on my face? Erm, my mask, I mean?"

"Mom, you go on ahead to the bus. I'll catch up!"

"Okay, if you're sure."

Midoriya stared some more and spoke.

"Um. Is that you...All Might?"

"Correctamundo, Midoriya, kid."

After quickly checking that they were good and

truly alone, All Might removed the black mask, revealing the face of his true form underneath.

"Knew it!" said Midoriya, eyes sparkling.

"Your classmates don't know about my true form, which is why I was the ideal teacher to play this part. Good old Aizawa coached me in the ways of villainy, too. Had me watch video clips, do all sorts of research… I was sure nobody'd figure it out."

"Nobody did! Well, not until you saved my mom, anyway. That's when I thought, 'This guy must be a hero.' Leaping into action like that, without hesitating, you know…? Plus, I know exactly how tall you are…"

"Ha ha, it's just in my nature. Leaping before looking."

"Anyway… Thanks so much for saving my mom," said Midoriya with a deep bow. He didn't rise back up.

"What's the matter, kid?"

Midoriya's voice quivered.

"It's just that… I'm not there yet. So much further to go… If you hadn't saved her, she'd be…"

Just the thought of his mother getting hurt was enough to make the boy feel inadequate. Undeserving.

"I was just overly hasty—a bad habit of mine. If I hadn't saved her, you'd have gotten the job done

yourself."

"But…"

"Humility's great, kid, but it's starting to get on my nerves!"

"Ack, that's the last thing I want, All Might!"

Midoriya raised his tear-filled eyes, and his mentor clapped his hands down on his student's shoulders with a smile.

"Ha ha! Just a little American joke, there!"

"Which part was American, exactly…?"

All Might grinned again, meaning to cheer up the whimpering Midoriya.

"Stay humble, but accept genuine praise when it comes your way. All joking aside, you were a force to be reckoned with today. You had the determination to save every last hostage, the composure to put together a strategy, and the leadership to get your friends working together… Tough enough to make any villain cry uncle, I'd say."

"Thanks, All Might!"

The barrage of compliments from his personal hero was enough to blow the dams of Midoriya's tear ducts, showering All Might with buckets' worth of emotion.

"Like I keep saying, we've got to do something about the crying, kid!"

"S-sorry!"

But no matter how hard Midoriya wanted to look the part of the hero, there was no stopping the torrent now.

Someday. Someday I'll hold back the tears and be a hero who saves people with nothing but a smile!

The sought-after smile crept onto the boy's face—a sign of all his heroics to come.

Epilogue

A man in an obvious hurry approached the front gate of U.A. High School. With bulging muscles, an intrepid scowl, and a beard of fire, Flame Hero: Endeavor was unmistakable. He also happened to be Todoroki's father.

But as he approached the gate, the thick automatic doors slammed shut.

"What...?"

No, not even a parent, famous hero, and alum could bypass U.A.'s security system without a student ID or an authorized guest pass.

"Open up! I'm missing Parents' Day!"

Knowing time was short, Endeavor pounded his fists against the doors. In one balled hand, he held a crumpled paper that read, PARENTS' DAY NOTICE. He'd only just discovered the notice, which must have fluttered under his desk when it popped out of his agency's fax machine. Given the family's dark history, Shoto Todoroki generally had as little to do with Endeavor as possible, so the father saw Parents' Day as an invaluable opportunity to check on the progress his creation was making.

Still pounding at the gate, Endeavor had a thought.

Maybe he *could get me in…*

'He' being the eternal thorn in Endeavor's side and U.A.'s newest educator, All Might. The top hero would have no trouble getting the gate open, but Endeavor's brow furrowed at the thought.

That buffoon left me the strangest voice mail a few days back…

He'd deleted the message immediately, of course. No, Endeavor wasn't about to go begging his hated rival for help, but there was soon no need, because the gate opened as if in answer to his prayers.

"Well, if it isn't Endeavor. How long has it been?"

It was U.A.'s school nurse, Youthful Hero: Recovery Girl. Contrary to her title, the elderly healer walked

with a syringe-shaped cane and had her hair tied up in a neat bun.

"Recovery Girl! Good to see you," said Endeavor, managing to mind his manners for someone he'd known nearly all his life.

"What brings you to us, today?"

"It's Par—"

He stopped himself. The number two hero couldn't very well admit that he'd taken time off to attend Parents' Day for his son. Wouldn't want anyone mistaking the ambitious, prideful Endeavor for a doting father. To start with, it simply wasn't true. In his mind, a hero had to project strength and nothing but. Especially not the image of a sensitive family man.

Endeavor cleared his throat a little more than necessary and corrected himself.

"Ahem… I just happened to be passing by. Thought I might drop in on my old alma mater…"

"Is that so?"

Endeavor was still anxious to catch the tail end of Parents' Day, but Recovery Girl seemed not to notice how antsy he was.

"Come to think of it, your boy's in the Hero Course, isn't he?"

"Right you are, Recovery Girl!"

Throwing him the cue he needed, she went on.

"Today is Parents' Day, you know? I hear class 1-A was fooled into thinking their mothers and fathers were taken hostage, as a trial of sorts. The children had to figure out how to save them."

"Sounds like an elaborate setup…"

Endeavor imagined his son performing admirably. His progeny, with Endeavor's superior genes and the ultimate Quirk, was sure to prove his mettle. The father had a sudden change of heart; observing those superior genetics in action was, in fact, his duty. Wanting to be here didn't necessarily make him a soft, doting daddy.

"Since I'm here, I might as well see how they're doing…"

"Oh, they're already done."

"What…?" spat Endeavor, stunned.

"It sounded like they had quite a tumultuous time."

"If only I hadn't found out so late!"

Recovery Girl grinned at Endeavor, who'd accidentally spilled the beans.

"Just passing by, were you? No need to lie. Besides, I spotted the notice in your hand."

Endeavor ignited the paper in a flash, destroying all evidence.

"Tut, tut. A hero mustn't use his Quirk for personal reasons, Endeavor."

"No clue what you're talking about, Recovery Girl. You sure you don't need glasses at your age?"

Recovery Girl was taken aback, and Endeavor's face stiffened.

Damn it all! If only that fax hadn't ended up under the desk!

Maybe, just maybe, his son's wish had come true.

A Note from the Creator

The novels are here! You'll get to read about the characters going about their everyday lives—something I haven't been able to squeeze much of into the manga, as I've been too focused on moving the plot forward. I really want to add more content like this into the manga itself. Maybe at some point!

KOHEI HORIKOSHI

A Note from the Author

I absolutely love *My Hero Academia*. I love it so
much that I worried whether or not people would
enjoy this novelization. Despite that unease, I had
a ton of fun writing it, so nothing would make me
happier than knowing that readers are enjoying it.

ANRI YOSHI

MY HERO ACADEMIA:
SCHOOL BRIEFS—PARENTS' DAY

Written by Anri Yoshi
Original story by Kohei Horikoshi
Cover and interior design by Shawn Carrico
Translation by Caleb Cook

BOKU NO HERO ACADEMIA YUUEI HAKUSHO © 2016 by Kohei Horikoshi, Anri Yoshi
All rights reserved.
First published in Japan in 2016 by SHUEISHA Inc., Tokyo.
English translation rights arranged by SHUEISHA Inc.

Published by VIZ Media, LLC
P.O. Box 77010
San Francisco, CA 94107

Library of Congress Cataloging-in-Publication Data

Names: Horikoshi, Kohei, 1986- author, artist. | Yoshi, Anri, contributor. |
    Cook, Caleb D., translator.
Title: Parents' day / Kohei Horikoshi, Anri Yoshi ; translation by Caleb Cook.
Description: San Francisco, CA : VIZ Media LLC, [2019] | Series: My hero
    academia: school briefs ; 1 | Summary: "The U.A. High School hero course
    teaches young hopefuls everything they need to become heroes. Between
    killer events like the sports festival and internships, there's even
    parents' day!"-- Provided by publisher.
Identifiers: LCCN 2018057424 | ISBN 9781974704866 (paperback)
Subjects: | CYAC: Heroes--Fiction. | High school--Fiction. |
    Schools--Fiction. | Ability--Fiction. | Fantasy. | BISAC: FICTION / Media
    Tie-In.
Classification: LCC PZ7.1.H6636 Par 2019 | DDC [Fic]--dc23
LC record available at https://lccn.loc.gov/2018057424

Printed in the U.S.A.

10 9 8 7 6 5 4 3 2 1
First printing, April 2019

viz.com

shonenjump.com